"I read in a book once," Bill said, "that the African elephant is untameable, highly dangerous—even when quite small."

Ginny's voice was dreamy as she stared at the baby elephant and said, "Untameable—it's absolutely adorable."

"If only he didn't spread his ears so," Bill said apprehensively. "It's unnerving."

"He's only waving," Ginny repled. "Just being friendly."

Bill Travers' caution and common sense had to give way before his wife's feeling that elephants, especially baby ones, could be lovable.

They behaved more like juvenile delinquents than like elephants. They trampled and uprooted the flower-beds; they splashed themselves and everyone else with liquid red mud; they trumpeted menacingly and poked their inquisitive trunks in everywhere.

"Absolutely adorable," Ginny sighed.

AN ELEPHANT CALLED
SLOWLY

ERNEST DUDLEY

*Based on a Screenplay
by Bill Travers and James Hill*

▲ *PYRAMID BOOKS*
NEW YORK

AN ELEPHANT CALLED SLOWLY

A PYRAMID BOOK
Published by arrangement with Lion International Films Ltd.

Pyramid edition published April 1970
Second printing, August 1970

Printed in the United States of America

PYRAMID BOOKS are published by Pyramid Publications
A Division of The Walter Reade Organization, Inc.
444 Madison Avenue, New York, New York 10022

Foreword

Virginia McKenna and Bill Travers, international film stars who are in private life Mr. and Mrs. Travers, have a wide friendship among wild animals. They worked with them in *Born Free* and *Ring of Bright Water,* two best-selling books that were turned into hit motion pictures. The African bush country seems like a second home to them and one they felt they would enjoy revisiting. Therefore they welcomed the suggestion of a friend to do a "spot of caretaking" at a bungalow in a remote part of East Africa.

Their only regret was that this time they could not take their children with them. When they filmed *Born Free* they took along their older children, but now those three—William, Louise and Justin—were at school, and the baby, Daniel, was just too young to make the trip—although he gives a winning performance in *An Elephant Called Slowly* in the scenes shot before they left their home in Surrey.

Photographed in color in Kenya, Tanzania and England, *An Elephant Called Slowly* was produced by Bill Travers and James Hill for Lion International Films Ltd., of England. Besides the Travers husband-wife team it features George Adamson and his lions of *Born Free* fame, and a supporting cast of elephants, rhinos, buffalo, giraffes, cheetahs, ostriches—a whole spectrum of wild life hunting, feeding, and playing in their natural habitat.

This novelization of *An Elephant Called Slowly* by author Ernest Dudley is a charming chronicle of the Travers safari and their unique "adoption" by a trio of amiable elephants—especially one called "Slowly."

This is how it happened.

Chapter 1

(1)

GINNY nudged her husband, who was fast asleep beside her. "That's Nairobi down below."

Bill woke up with a start.

"What—er—where?"

"There."

They glanced down at Nairobi Airport. It looked like a collection of matchboxes arranged on a green and yellow carpet. Bright sunshine contrasted vividly with the grey murk of Heathrow Airport, now far behind. They were arriving in another world. Africa.

"Look," Ginny said. "There's someone waving to us."

Bill gave her an old-fashioned look.

"Oh, good," he said.

Ginny shrugged her slim shoulders. All right, if he didn't believe her.

Bill settled himself to go back to sleep again, and while the VC-10 aimed itself at the airport below, Ginny thought what a different world this was from the snow-covered hills of Surrey they had left behind not long ago.

It was strange, she mused, once you have been to Africa you always have a longing to go back. The urge to return was irresistible, and any excuse would do, however flimsy. Even the mention of the name, as Bill said, sent a shiver of anticipatory delight through you. In this case the adventure had been started off by something quite small.

It was a letter which simply said: "So am off to Switzerland for three or four weeks, only a minor operation. Varicose veins, very boring. But how about a spot of caretaking while I am away? You and Bill would love it, I know; the place is full of characters."

Tom Woodson, from whom the letter had come, must have meant "character," Ginny thought, not "characters."

She had asked Bill at the time, "Where exactly is Tom's house?"

"It's in a remote part of—"

"I know, darling," she interrupted him. "It's in a remote part—it's in the letter—but where exactly is the house?"

"I think you turn left out of Nairobi," he replied.

Ginny glanced at him. "Oh, that's easy, isn't it?"

"Then you fork left," Bill went on enthusiastically. "Then you go on for about a hundred and fifty miles, and then fork right," he added helpfully.

Ginny said, "Mmm—can't go wrong, can we?"

"No," Bill said.

The only one who hadn't been excited about the trip was Henry, who was to drive them to the airport in the vintage Rolls Royce. He knew that for all its exterior opulence you could not rely on it in an emergency—it was just too old. In the drive outside the Travers cottage on the slopes of the Surrey hills, he stamped his feet, blew on his fingers and sounded the horn again and again. But the only response he got was the arrival at full speed of a spaniel, a sheep dog, and a poodle, the Travers family's dogs.

Henry distinctly disliked dogs, and they knew it. He jumped into the venerable Rolls and wound up the window. As the dogs barked and snarled at him, he snarled back. He didn't get out again even when Bill and Ginny Travers finally appeared, laden down with luggage. He did lower the window enough to wish them a good morning and ask Bill if he could manage.

"Yes, I think so, thank you, Henry."

Henry straightened himself in his seat. "Where to this time, Mr. T?"

"Back to Africa again."

Henry cocked an eye up at the chilly, leaden sky. "What a shame—all that 'orrible nice warm sunshine."

(2)

Ginny looked out now at all that sunshine, but her thoughts were still back in Surrey, with the children. William, Louise and Justin were away at school, but Daniel, the youngest, had watched the departure from the sitting-room window, with Nanny behind him, his nose pressed against the pane. Ginny and Bill had decided that he was too young to go with them.

When they had made the film, *Born Free,* William, Louise and Justin had accompanied them to Africa. There had been no Daniel then, and their decision to take their three children had been arrived at after a great deal of soul searching. Some people had been rather surprised that they should have taken them on an adventure which might have proved very hazardous. At the time there were alarming stories of trouble in Kenya; there were problems of food and water, insects and wild animals.

But as Ginny and her husband said, the children were part of their lives, part of their joys and sorrows, their comfort and pain, and wouldn't they be selfish to deny them this wonderful experience? However, it was different with Daniel. He was far too young to take on the journey, and so they must leave him behind with Nanny.

In the car she had turned to Bill and pointed to Daniel at the window. "Look at the little angel," she said.

Bill looked back in time to observe a change in the "little angel's" expression, as he blew a raspberry at them.

And at that moment they had driven off.

It was when they were about five miles from Heathrow Airport that the Rolls broke down. The opportune arrival of a lorry driver who recognized Bill Travers and Virginia McKenna saved the day. In no time at all he had got the old Rolls in tow, and with Henry sitting at the wheel, trying to look as dignified as he possibly could under the circumstances, they were heading in the direction of London once more.

"Do you think we'll make it?" Ginny asked her husband.

Bill looked at his watch and considered the question carefully. "I reckon we'll just miss it by twenty seconds," he replied.

"Oh," Ginny said. "Perhaps your watch is fast?"

"Shh," he said. As she glanced at him in surprise he continued: "Listen—you can almost hear the clock ticking."

Ginny looked at the clock on the dashboard.

"Yes!" she said. "You *can* almost hear the clock ticking."

(3)

Over the airport loudspeakers at Heathrow the announcer was apologising for the delay in the departure of the East Africa Airways VC-10 flight to Nairobi. It was owing to, as he put it, "circumstances beyond our control."

The VC-10 lifted up into the grey English skies, its nose pointed toward Africa. Bill Travers turned to his wife with a smile of self-congratulation. "Rather lucky for us, wasn't it?"

"Lucky?" She regarded him with astonishment. "What do you mean, 'lucky'?"

"I mean that there were circumstances beyond the airport's control which held up the plane."

"We were the circumstances," she told him firmly.

"Oh," he said.

"Really," Ginny said to him, and they both relaxed in their seats and began thinking about what lay ahead.

Chapter 2

(1)

As they made their way down the aircraft's gangway, the announcer's voice over the loudspeaker reached them. "East African Airways are happy to announce the arrival of their flight from London."

They gazed ahead at the groups of Europeans and Africans beyond the tarmac, who were watching the arrival of the plane. On the flat roof of the aircraft building there was another waiting crowd above the name NAIROBI AIRPORT in large letters.

Suddenly Ginny pointed straight ahead.

"Look, there he is," she said. "I told you."

Bill stared in the direction she was pointing and then back to her.

"Who?"

"The man who was waving at us," Ginny said.

There was in fact a short, wiry figure in a kind of uniform, with African trimmings, waving excitedly. He wore horn-rimmed spectacles and was jigging up and down in his efforts to attract the attention of somebody disembarking from the aircraft. But Bill didn't think he was waving at them.

"Not us. He's not waving at us. Must be somebody else."

"I'm sure it's us," Ginny replied.

Sure enough, a few moments later, they caught sight of the little man again. He saw them and rushed up, still waving frantically.

"Over here," he shouted, grinning widely. "This way, this way." He turned round a corner of the airport building.

Ginny and Bill detached themselves from the crowd and followed him. Now they stood and gazed at him uncomprehendingly. He was dancing as if the sight of them was heaven-sent; he grinned more broadly than ever, although it did little to remove the impression he gave that he was rather a shabby character.

"I recognised you," he chattered. "I recognise you from the last time you were here. Welcome back!" he cried. "Welcome back, welcome to Kenya."

"Thank you," Bill said.

"Doubtless you are now very happy?" the little man asked earnestly. His horn-rims glinted in the sunshine.

"Yes," Bill replied, "very happy."

"Very happy," Ginny said. "It's wonderful to be back in this lovely country."

Already the spell of Africa held her in its grip.

She glanced at her husband and she could tell by the lift of his shoulders as he sniffed the air that he was experiencing the same emotions that she felt. The very atmosphere tingled with excitement. It wasn't only the colourful clothes that could be seen all around and the excitable chatter of strange tongues—there was a sense of welcome in the brilliant sunshine. It was as if the very heart of Africa were opening out for you.

The little man beamed as if he personally owned every inch of the entire land of Kenya.

"I am Mopagee," he announced himself. "A.1. Luxurious Tours—" He broke off as if Bill knew precisely what he was talking about, and he had no need to add anything further.

Ginny glanced at her husband with a little frown of puzzlement.

"Ah, yes," Bill was saying, with a nod of understanding.

"Your transport is waiting," Mr. Mopagee said. "Please return it in the same good condition at the end of the safari."

Now Ginny glanced at Bill with mounting admiration.

"I didn't know you had arranged all this, darling," she said warmly. "It's terribly organised of you."

Her husband stuck out his chest proudly, and then said, with a modest grin, "Well, I just kept it as a little surprise. I simply wrote, hired a vehicle for a month—in good condition—"

Mr. Mopagee butted in, handing him a large, official-looking book to sign. Bill did so, whereupn Mr. Mopagee handed the book to Ginny. She glanced at it with surprise.

"Oh, me?" For some reason she felt flattered that she had to sign, too. He was rather a nice little man, really.

"Just a minute." She signed where Mr. Mopagee's finger indicated. He then handed Bill the car key which had a large tag attached to it.

Bill explained to his wife: "We pay twenty shillings a day in advance. The oil and all petrol, of course, are our responsibility."

She nodded, then turned to say something agreeable to Mr. Mopagee. But he had vanished. She spun round and thought she caught a glimpse of him as he disappeared round the corner of the building.

It occurred to her that his movements had become somewhat furtive, his eyes, behind his horn-rims, full of cunning triumph. She gave a look at Bill who was frowning a little at the car key he held. Then he picked up his suitcases, she picked up hers and followed him as he strode off.

A few moments later they were staring with dismay at a landrover, the number plate of which read CU 4662. Bill looked at his key-tag—CU 4662.

It looked hideous, a relic of some ill-fated safari of many years ago. Battered and painted like a zebra in yellow and black stripes, it bore trophies of long-forgotten hunting expeditions in the shape of impala horns tied to its battered bonnet. On one corner of the windscreen was still scrawled: Lot 5.

Bill and Ginny let their baggage fall and with slumped shoulders stared at the dismal-looking wreck before them.

"Was the paintwork thrown in for twenty shillings a day?" Ginny couldn't resist asking her husband.

"Hired as seen," he replied, in lugubrious tones.

"Seen to be believed," she said. And then she sheered up, and though it was with an effort, her face brightened and she said, "Oh well, it's different, darling. It's, it's—different. Let's go."

The decrepit vehicle rattled and shook as Ginny and Bill got into it. She sat beside him as he looked doubtfully at the dashboard. He tried to start the car—unsuccessfully.

He got out and lifted the bonnet, his head going underneath it and then recoiling as he stared at the engine. It was liberally smothered with red dust and looked a pretty hopeless proposition. His heart sank as he stared at the landover's innards.

"Mr. Mopagee," he muttered bitterly.

Ginny, for want of something better to do, was jiggling the key, and as Bill muttered the little man's name the engine suddenly leapt into life.

Bill's eyes popped with surprise and excitement.

"Mr. Mopagee," he exclaimed triumphantly.

Obviously the name had some magical impact upon the landrover. Hurriedly he slammed down the bonnet and, not giving the engine a chance to change its mind and pack up, he scrambled back into the car, gave his wife a smile which could only be described as smug, and drove off.

Ginny wore a smile of her own which might also best be described as smug, for she was fully under the impression that the engine had started as a result of her jiggling the key. However, she thought it wiser to let her husband take the credit. It would encourage him.

"Well done, darling," she said. "What was it?" she asked, her smile changing to one of innocence.

"Oh, nothing," he replied airily. "Nothing at all."

She smiled back at him and, picking up a duster from under the dashboard, made as if to polish the window in front of her. To her surprise, however, hand and duster went right through. The window, in fact, wasn't there. With a slightly embarrassed giggle she replaced the duster under the dash.

(2)

Outside a grocery store in Nairobi's busy town center Bill stopped the landrover and hopped out. Ginny looked at him questioningly.

"Stock up with food," he said cryptically and hurried into the store. He reappeared with a cardboard packing case labelled "Beans," followed by some Africans also carrying large cardboard packing cases similarly labelled.

"Not more beans?" Ginny queried, as she turned from observing his load to the Africans with theirs.

"Come in very useful," he replied.

"Six cases?"

She had counted them as they were being loaded into the back of the vehicle.

"Absolutely vital," he assured her.

"Yes, darling," she said.

Bill disappeared back into the store while she got out of the car and helped the Africans load the last case of beans. He reappeared with a large bunch of green bananas which were stowed on top of the beans.

Ginny watched him curiously as he went round to the front of the bonnet and opened it. She got back into the landrover, reached forward and began jiggling the ignition key. Meanwhile, Bill was addressing the dust-covered vehicle.

"Mr. Mopagee," he declaimed.

At once the engine gave a cough and began turning over exactly as had happened before. In Bill's mind there was no doubt that all that was required to start the landrover were the magic words: "Mr. Mopagee."

He clambered back into the driving seat and smiled, still somewhat smugly, at Ginny. She replied with a smile of almost equal smugness, quite convinced in her mind that she had solved the problem of starting the engine. It was simply a matter of jiggling the ignition key. The feminine touch.

They drove under the jacaranda trees in the main street and then presently Nàirobi was behind them. They headed along a country road below the mountains, which stood green and majestic against a bright blue sky filled with typical, fleecy white clouds. It was a brilliant day and Ginny thought how it all looked just the same. The old excitement rushed back as she remembered how it had looked when she had first seen it, with the same violet mountains in the distance. Brightly coloured birds flew up, startled into shrill cries, as the landrover rattled on. Yes, there was a roller, pale blue and lilac, perched on a bush—and there, slinking along the reddish, dusty road, was a lone jackal, furtive and sinister, just as she had seen one the last time she was in Africa.

Now the clouds were rolling in banks, deepening in the distance into purple and ebony. And she recalled, as she watched them, how these clouds never seemed to obscure the sun. She remembered how she had loved the clouds.

Her thoughts went back to Dorking, where the snow would be lying on the ground and the skies would be grey and overcast with more snow to come.

Bill had bought some picture postcards at the grocery store, and she promised herself that as soon as she could she would send them back to Daniel and to the children at school.

She knew that William, Louise and Justin would be longing to hear news of Africa and what it was like to her and their father on this return visit. For they, like Ginny and Bill, had fallen under Africa's spell when they had been there during the filming of *Born Free*. They, too, longed to return.

As they sped along the yellowish-red lava-dust track, they saw a cloud of dust approaching on the horizon. They soon made out a Volkswagen mini-bus. The cloud grew larger and larger. Now the minibus was upon them. Now it was sweeping past them, almost indiscernible in the great dust cloud that enveloped it, and which now enveloped Ginny and Bill.

Coughing and choking, Bill managed to keep the vehicle on the road as they headed onwards. As the dust cleared, he turned towards Ginny and was surprised to see her wearing a pair of goggles. She was reaching for another pair under the dashboard and handed them to Bill.

"A.1. Luxurious Tours, sir," she said.

Bill grinned and grabbed the goggles, pulling them over his head as they sped on, with a loud bang from the exhaust as if Mr. Mopagee himself were making a comment upon the Volkswagen which was now a lava-dust cloud receding into the distance.

Chapter 3

(1)

Now they were approaching a river with luxuriantly green grass everywhere, and shady trees and dense undergrowth extending along the river bank. Bill drew to a stop under a vast tree, its branches reaching out like a huge dark green umbrella. Steam was coming out of the landrover's bonnet as he and Ginny got out and looked across in the direction of the river.

"I hope 'Mr. Mopagee' is all right," Ginny said, indicating the bonnet.

Bill glanced at the steam which was by now almost obscuring the vehicle.

"Just a bit steamed up, I think."

Ginny turned away and gave a deep sigh.

"What a wonderful place for a swim," she said.

"And for a nice tin of beans," Bill said, and Ginny laughed.

In the undergrowth king-fishers and other birds were singing, and Bill and Ginny went back to the landrover. Bill pulled out one of the cases of baked beans, while Ginny took off her clothes, shook the dust out of them, went down to the river and plunged in. Bill made a hearty meal. Cooked or uncooked, beans were just as delicious.

Presently, Ginny, draped in a bright blue bath-towel, was standing beside him as he lay stretched out on the grass.

"Oh, it's so marvellous to be back in Africa," Ginny said. "Everything is so beautiful and peaceful." She looked up overhead. "Look at the clouds."

Bill had sat up, and was gazing intently, not at the clouds, or even at her, but at the surface of the river.

"And look at that funny ripple in the river," he said.

Ginny gave a start and swung round. There was a crocodile emerging with a soft plop from the swiftly-flowing river and sliding slowly up the river bank in the direction of a bird which was standing on a sand bank. The river was open at this point, with no trees.

"Do you think it's been there all the time?" Ginny said, and shivered.

Bill did not answer. His attention remained rivetted on the crocodile, and it occurred to him that there might be others lower down on the river bank.

He knew that crocodiles are not so ravenous as they are often made out to be, though their appearance is dangerous. Owing to the way in which its jawbones are arranged a crocodile can't chew its food, it can only hold it in its mouth. It will seize an animal drinking at the river's edge, and drag it under to drown it. Then it will keep the victim in its lair until it has decomposed, then cut it into pieces with its shear-like jaws.

The damage done by crocodiles is small, but they have been slaughtered almost out of existence in many areas, and the time is fast approaching when they will need protection as do so many wild animals, in the process of being wiped out by indiscriminate slaughter.

Although it is a lethargic creature it can move like lightning if occasion demands, and Bill found the thought irresistible, that this might be one of the occasions.

"I think we should push off," he said, "while the going's good."

Ginny glanced at him. "I think you're probably right. Poor crocodile."

"Why so poor?" her husband queried.

Ginny said it made her feel sick to know that one reason for the destruction of the crocodiles was that their skins were highly prized by hunters. She was interrupted by a movement she had detected in the bush.

"Don't look now," she said, "but I think there's something over there—."

"Just because you see a croc in the river you immediately think the place is alive with—"

Bill broke off. There appeared in the green undergrowth at the place where Ginny was staring a pair of aggressive-looking horns. Even as Bill's gaze became glued to the spot, the dark leaves suddenly became a frame for a great, horned, black head.

"Buffalo," muttered Ginny.

"Buffalo?" Bill tried to make his voice sound as casual as possible. "They can be very bad-tempered you know."

Even animal-poachers, Bill knew, liked to keep clear of buffalo, owing to its reputation of being Africa's most dangerous animal. Not that they are aggressive—left alone, they graze just like any domestic cattle. But if injured or frightened, and they have suffered a certain amount of persecution by man, then buffalo will attack. And a formidable enemy it can be. The lion, for example, thinks twice before taking on a buffalo.

Bill and Ginny began collecting the remains of the picnic, Bill keeping one eye on the buffalo and the other on the landrover several yards away. Too many yards away, it seemed to him.

"I think we ought to go and see if "Mr. Mopagee's' cooled off," he said.

Ginny was already heading in the vehicle's direction. She glanced back and pointed to the picnic-basket which Bill had forgotten to pick up.

"You've forgotten the basket," Ginny was saying.

"Do we need it?" Bill groaned. The buffalo was still watching him from beneath wide, horned brows.

"Of course," Ginny said.

She was already proceeding to get into the landrover. Bill had to reach a quick decision and gauge the chance he had of getting to the picnic-basket before the buffalo got him. Assuming, of course, that the buffalo's intention was to get him.

Bill eyed the dark shape half hidden in the bushes. He reckoned that the animal must stand over five feet at the shoulders and weighed something like 2,000 pounds. If it did happen to be in a less than happy mood and took a dislike to him, he needed to get out of its way. Pronto. He decided that he could just about get the basket, and with a quick dash he snatched it up then rushed to the landrover.

He was making fast time getting into the vehicle when he remembered that there was a certain ritual to be gone through. Quickly he got out and hurried around to the bonnet. Perhaps it wasn't necessary to lift it, he decided. He uttered the magic words: "Mr. Mopagee!"

Too late. The horns moved menacingly towards him. Desperately, not knowing whether to run or face up to the advancing beast, Bill turned, hesitated; then—but it wasn't necessary to run or stay, after all. Emerging from the bushes was no savage buffalo, but an innocent-looking cow, urged forward by its grinning native drover.

"*Jambo, bwana!*" he called out cheerfully, ambling off into the undergrowth after the cow.

Bill's mingled relief and astonishment was interrupted by a burst of laughter from Ginny.

"Our first taste of wild-life," she cried.

Bill managed a wan grin, and climbed into the landrover.

(2)

They were driving along under the thorn trees, when they rounded a clump of reeds and across open country Ginny caught sight of a herd of wildebeest, grey-coloured, reminding her somehow of Highland cattle, only they had longer legs. Ginny knew that somewhere on the fringes of the wildebeest there would be lurking lions and leopards, hyenas and jackals, always on the watch, ready to grab a straying calf or attack a mother in labour. And somewhere, too, high above, the vultures would wheel, ready also to swoop and feed on any remains of a wildebeest victim left behind by the predators.

Then, in the distance, a herd of zebras put in an appearance. Here, in their wild state, zebras lived, not like some oddly striped black and white horse in a zoo, but as an integral part of their homeland. Like the wildebeest, often called the clown of Africa, because of its capacity for looking sometimes comical, sometimes frightening, the zebra is as harmless and inoffensive as the most peaceful dove, relying on speedy retreat as its best defence in case of danger.

Ginny remembred being warned that if one was afflicted with even the mildest form of astigmatism, to look at a herd of zebras at close quarters when they were on the move—especially through a heat haze—could produce a most uncomfortable sensation—that was what made zebras so difficult to count, to anyone whose eyesight wasn't perfect!

Ginny knew that at last she really was in Africa. It seemed to her that it was like one's youth. Africa can be revisited, but it could never be recaptured. Her eyes ranged the landscape; in the bush country she could see the giraffes, pausing as they moved along to eat from the tops of bushes and trees. Their great height enabled them to get at the topmost and tenderest shoots and leaves, which other animals couldn't reach. Their movements were deliberate, waving and graceful, because of the curious way they were constructed. Their bodies so short, their neck so grotesquely long and their elongated legs. The tallest living mammal, they were. Ginny recalled being told that a giraffe's lung capacity was less than half that of a horse. About twenty pints of air—which was why, despite its long legs, it wouldn't stand a chance in a race against a horse.

Then, a saddleback stork moved through the long grass. At the same time a herd of buffalo, a great black mass, came running across the track in front of the landrover, so that Bill was forced to stop with a screech of brakes.

"Not a vehicle in sight," Ginny said, "and here we are in the middle of a traffic jam."

"Can't win," Bill said. "Everyone's against the motorist."

He pointed to a signboard stuck upon a post which read: ANIMALS HAVE THE RIGHT OF WAY.

Now an ostrich, with young babies, appeared and headed off down the track. More buffalo moved in the bushes; one of them lumbered across, narrowly missing the front of the landrover, so that Ginny and Bill could see the tick birds, or ox-peckers, on its back. Looking like over-large star-lings, with curved, sharply-pointed claws by which they cling to animals' hides without slipping off, they feed on the ticks which infest buffalo, zebra and especially rhino.

Those adult ticks which are found on rhino lay their eggs on the skin of the ears, neck and shoul-ders of their host. They provide succulent food for the tick birds.

Now the track was clear again, and made a sort of sandy ribbon through green bush country with the lofty purple mountains in the background.

A signpost came into view with an arrow point-ing and the legend: NAIROBI 150 MILES.

"Hundred and fifty miles," Ginny cried. By now Bill was stepping on the accelerator as hard as he dared. They came to a fork in the road, and he was about to take the left fork when he was corrected by his wife.

"Hey, right," she shouted.

"Whoops," and Bill swung the car onto the right fork.

The road became less and less a permanent track, almost disappearing in places, and completely vanishing when it crossed a dried-up stream. Bill and Ginny had not seen any sign of habitation for some time, when at last they passed a tree with a buffalo skull nailed onto the trunk as they headed along the now dusty red track. It was obviously intended to be a sign that they were approaching some place—a camp, perhaps; or a house, someone's home.

Then they saw the bungalow. It lay over to their right and they could see an old London bus converted into a motor-caravan beside it. But both their faces dropped with disappointment as they realized at once that it must be inhabited. Someone was actually living there, it appeared quite obvious.

"This can't be it," Ginny said. "Someone's living there."

Bill nodded with understanding sympathy. Tom Woodson's house must be still further on. The bungalow looked spick and span with the doors and the windows wide open. Flowers bloomed colourfully on either side of the path and underneath the windows.

Ginny had been standing up with her head through the landrover's roof, but now, her expression dejected, she sat down again beside Bill and he drove on. She couldn't understand how they had come to make such a mistake. She felt certain she had been correct when she had told Bill to fork right, when he had been about to take the left fork.

Perhaps there was another fork in the road ahead which would get them onto the right track.

They had not gone very far, however, when the track, rough as it was, suddenly ended.

They were in bush country, and the landrover halted by a tree with the bush all around, and the purple mountains beyond. It was all very lovely, very peaceful, the silence broken only by bird-song —but they still hadn't found Tom Woodson's home.

"What's wrong?" Ginny asked.

"I think I ought to tell you," Bill said, as he stood up through the rolled-back canvas roof and gazed around, "that we have just run out of road."

Chapter 4

(1)

BILL stood looking at the vast panorama of uninhabited African bush ahead of him as Ginny sat down again in the driving seat.

"Well, ask someone the way," Ginny said. "Don't just stand there."

Bill looked at those miles of African bush ahead, then he sat down beside Ginny. He glanced at her and then got out of the car and closed the door with great deliberation.

"Where are you going?" Ginny wanted to know.

Bill said, with great dignity: "To ask someone the way," and he headed off in the direction of the bungalow about fifty yards behind them.

Ginny leaned out of the car to watch him as he stalked off, then, with a smile on her face she got out of the car herself and with equal deliberation set off after him. After a few moments she had to quicken her pace and it ended with her running after him.

He had reached the front of the bungalow, where the flowers grew in abundance on either side of the entrance. There was a thatched roof over a sort of verandah, with walls some four feet high in front. Beyond was a green door to the enclosed part of the house.

Bill called out: "Hodi"—he was rather proud of his knowledge of Swahili, however limited it was in reality. There was no reply.

"Anyone there—anyone at home?" he called again, but there was still no reply. Ginny gave him a quick look and then went cautiously through the front door into the bungalow. On a table she saw an envelope. It was the same colour as the one she had received from Tom Woodson! She picked it up, calling to Bill.

"Look, it's for us."

"What is?" Bill said, coming into the bungalow. Ginny turned to him and waved the letter.

"It's from Tom." She was reading it as Bill joined her and without looking up she said: "We're here—this is it."

She finished the letter, putting it back into the envelope and pushed it into her pocket. "The key is under the flowerpot," she said and she hurried outside to the flower-covered entrance. There were several pots of flowers on the verandah wall, and after lifting the third she found the key underneath.

As she came back into the bungalow Bill was waiting by the open door, a puzzled expression on his face. He said: "Terribly sorry, but I don't understand." He glanced at the key she was holding. "The door was already open, so what do we need the key for?"

Ginny looked thoughtfully at the key she was holding. "Yes, well—I wonder what this is for?" she said.

A thought occurred to her and she hurried out to the long green-coloured motor-caravan beside the bungalow. It was, in fact, an old bus converted, and she found a bolt on the back-door with a padlock on it. The padlock yielded at once to the key.

She pulled open the doors to reveal the kitchen interior. She called over her shoulder to Bill in astonishment: "A kitchen in a bus."

Bill came out of the bungalow, saw the kitchen but pretended to take it all as a matter of course. What was so eccentric about a kitchen in a bus? It was quite a good kitchen, as kitchens in buses went; and anyway, this wasn't dear old rural Surrey, this was wildest Africa. Where anything could happen, and frequently did.

It was now late afternoon and while Bill began shifting the baggage from the landrover into the bungalow, Ginny started to prepare the evening's supper. She found some potatoes, and began peeling them. While she sat there she glanced round about her and sighed happily. Two hornbills watched her from a tree, and then a little further on she could see a ground squirrel nibbling away. Then on the wall which Tom Woodson had built to shelter part of the garden were two geckos. As she drank in the scene with all its beauty and peace, she saw two more different kinds of geckos or lizards, one blue and orange, one green and grey, on a nearby rock.

She heard Bill grunting a bit with the exertion of shifting the baggage and put down the bowl and potatoes. She went to see if she could give a hand, but by now he seemed to have removed all the baggage and had turned his attention to the heavy cases of baked beans.

Ginny went back to her potatoes and resumed peeling them.

Bill appeared, staggering underneath a large carton labelled "48 tins of baked beans in tomato sauce." She had to laugh at the way in which he was being careful not to trip over the flower-beds. He made his way to the bungalow, then he paused to poke his head from behind the carton. Ginny smiled at him.

"Phew," Bill groaned. "Well, don't laugh—they're heavy."

Ginny said lightly: "Put them in that cupboard, darling." She indicated the cupboard inside the kitchen.

Balancing the large carton carefully, Bill mounted the bus-steps and somehow got himself into the kitchen. He placed the packages on the floor and turned to the cupboard which Ginny had indicated.

He opened it, only to step back with a groan of dismay. A whole array of tins of baked beans were packed inside the cupboard. Several tins fell out as Bill opened the door. Tacked to the edge of the shelf was a scribbled note. "In case you run short. Tom."

Bill replaced the tins in the cupboard with a heavy sigh, and closed the door.

He then proceeded to stack the cases at the side of the caravan, making the journey to and fro without a word to Ginny. His wife peeled away at the potatoes. The squirrel nibbled at some nuts, the lizards on the wall basked in the afternoon sun, and the lizards on the rocks lay quiet, their hooded eyes closed.

His task completed, Bill went into the bungalow. In the tiny bedroom he stood staring at the single bed with its mosquito-net above it. It wasn't big enough to sleep two, that was certain. He felt a movement by his shoulder and turned to face Ginny. With a smile and a nod at the bed he said to her: "Oh, of course, you must have it."

"Oh, no," she replied quickly, "you have it."

Bill started to protest that he couldn't possibly take the only bed in the place, but his wife interrupted him.

"Oh, no, I mean it," she insisted—"you've been driving all day."

"Oh, well," Bill said. "If you insist."

He moved to the bed and stretched himself out on it luxuriously, covering every inch of it. It felt extremely comfortable, and he closed his eyes as if prepared there and then to take a quick nap.

Ginny's attitude completely changed. She no longer radiated all sweetness and light. She glared at him.

"You don't mean it—you wouldn't—?" she choked.

Bill, still with his eyes closed, enjoying the luxury of the bed, answered sleepily. He barely restrained a yawn.

"Why not? You insisted," he reminded her.

Ginny pulled the door to with a slam and went out of the bungalow, muttering something about the selfishness of some husbands.

She searched the caravan kitchen for a frying pan in which to cook some sausages.

She made no comment as presently Bill emerged, whistling softly to himself and began removing the cardboard cases containing the baked beans from the caravan. Back in the bedroom, he finished positioning the cases. He surveyed the arrangement for a few moments, then he took one of the two mattresses off the lone bed and spread it on the cases. It would work, he decided, reasonably satisfactorily, and he was rewarded by Ginny appearing at the bedroom window.

What had Bill been up to, she had been wondering, removing all those baked beans out of the kitchen-cupboard? Her curiosity had finally overcome her annoyance at his selfishness about the only bed. She was clutching the frying-pan, the sausages still sizzling away, as she saw what he had devised.

"Oh, how very clever," she said. Her tone was more mollified now.

He grinned at her.

"I told you they would come in useful," he said, as he patted the mattress into place over the cases of baked beans.

He was answered by a horrified scream.

Ginny's smile of forgiveness had broken off as she glanced down at her shoes. Safari ants were crawling all over them.

"Ants!" she screamed. "Oh, oh, ants!"

She dashed into the bungalow, stamping her feet as if executing some tribal dance, in an effort to shake off the ants. Then she shot into the bedroom, where she handed the frying-pan, sausages still sizzling, to Bill. He took them automatically. He sat there, on his bed, while Ginny threw herself on to the other bed and began frantically pulling off her shoes.

"How very thoughtful," Bill said dryly. "Supper in bed."

And he proceeded to turn the sausages as they sizzled appetizingly in the pan.

Chapter 5

(1)

THE trees beside the bungalow made a dark, heavy green silhouette against the pink and golden sunrise. In the bedroom of Tom Woodson's bungalow, Bill was lying asleep on his do-it-yourself bed; next to him, in her bed, under the mosquito net, Ginny slept soundly.

Bill did not hear the scuffling noise and knocking outside the bungalow, but his wife heard it in her sleep and smiled dreamily. The knocking noise was repeated. Bill was half awake and grunted a query, but Ginny talked in her sleep.

"Come in."

Bill glanced at her. "Huh? What do you mean 'come in'?"

Ginny woke with a start. "Huh?" She stared at him uncomprehendingly. "Oh. Oh, I was dreaming I was in Kenya."

"Well," Bill reassured her, "you are."

"I know," Ginny replied, stifling a yawn. "But I was dreaming I was in a beautiful hotel by the silver sands, by the sea."

Bill eyed her for a moment. "You were definitely dreaming," he said.

But she was continuing with her dream. "Breakfast had just arrived. The waiter was just knocking at the door—"

Again that strange, muffled knock outside the bungalow.

Ginny stared at Bill.

"There you are," she said, and glanced again in the direction of the bedroom door. "Come in."

Bill, with a mighty yawn, and his face settling into a frown of curiosity, got out of bed and moved towards the window. He drew back a chink in the curtains and squinted through it. There was another scuffling noise outside.

As the curtains parted Ginny, behind him, let out a blood-curdling scream. Bill jumped back to stare at her open-mouthed. She was sitting up in bed, the mosquito-net wrapped round her neck.

"Ssh," Bill told her.

"What on earth was that?" she squeaked at him, her blue eyes wide with fright.

Bill turned with a glance at the gap in the curtain. "I don't know," he said slowly. He paused. Then he squared his shoulders. "I am about to investigate."

He turned back to the curtains and drew them wider. As he did so he gave an exclamation.

"Ooh!"

A large elephant's head filled his view. Hastily Bill closed the curtains.

"What is it?" Ginny said. Her voice was calmer.

Bill gave a gulp. He sat beside her on the bed.

"An elephant."

"I don't believe you."

Bill gave a shrug, tried to appear as nonchalant as he could. It wasn't a successful effort.

"Look—er—l-l-look for yourself."

"How—er—how?" She broke off, furious with herself for catching Bill's hesitant style of utterance. "How big?"

"Enormous."

Ginny stared, first at him disbelievingly, then at the closed curtains. She got up and crossed to the window. Slowly she pulled back the curtain to allow a tiny chink through which she could look. She paused, and then let the curtain fall back into place. She turned to Bill with a sympathetic smile.

"I'll get you some nice coffee," she said. "Strong," she emphasized, and went out of the bedroom.

Bill goggled after her. He scowled to himself, then very slowly got off the bed and went to the window. He paused, took a deep breath, and then drew back the curtains. He gazed at the landscape surrounding the bungalow, taking in the bush and forest beyond—there was no sign of any elephant.

He was still staring out of the window, puzzled, when he heard Ginny's voice. It seemed impossible that it was not an elephant he had seen taking up, as it seemed to him at that moment, the entire landscape. His speculations were interrupted by Ginny's sweet voice from the kitchen again.

"Bill, could you spare a moment?"

Ginny was standing gazing out across the verandah. Bill joined her, and he too gazed out at the area of grass and trees which was behind the bungalow. He found himself looking at a very small elephant.

He could hardly believe his eyes. He had to offer some sort of explanation. He said to his wife:

"It's larger close to."

Ginny smiled at him with maddening understanding. "You really do exaggerate things."

The tiny elephant turned its head, and with a wave of its trunk began walking toward them.

Ginny's voice was full of love and affection as she said, somewhat obviously, Bill thought: "Oh, look, it's coming toward us."

The elephant reached the door. Bill backed away slightly.

Ginny looked with delighted fascination as it approached while Bill continued to watch it with a slight air of nervousness. The elephant reached the bungalow door. It's tiny trunk came in through the doorway and began taking some fruit from a dish on the table. Bill stepped back, while Ginny's face was still filled with wonderment and fascinated awe at the sight of this little animal. Unafraid and perfectly at home, its trunk reached further still into the verandah, searching, and then found the fruit on the table.

"I read in a book once," Bill said, quickly backing away another yard, "that the African elephant is untamable, highly dangerous—even when quite small," he added emphatically.

Ginny's voice was quite dreamy as she still stared at the baby elephant and said: "Untamable—it's absolutely adorable."

The fruit had now disappeared entirely from the dish, and the baby elephant withdrew its trunk. It turned and started to move away as Bill and Ginny watched it. Bill was looking slightly more confident, then, beyond it, they saw something else—this time a very much larger elephant. The big elephant was moving very quickly, trumpeting deafeningly. In only a matter of seconds its huge trunk was reaching into the bungalow.

Ginny stared at Bill, the light of love and fascination had vanished from her eyes. Now her face was filled with alarm. Bill's reaction was immediate, he gave her a push ahead of him as they dashed for the bedroom and slammed the door.

Bill gave a quick look out of the window. Yet another enormous elephant was advancing upon the bungalow. Even as he stared at it, his jaw sagging with mingled dismay and astonishment, the second enormous elephant approached; it, too, trumpeted loudly. He quickly turned back to Ginny and together they began heaping all the furniture they could find against the bedroom door.

"And I'm not even dressed," Bill heard himself muttering.

"It's all right," Ginny reassured him. "I don't think they noticed."

They could hear both elephants trumpeting away, interspersed with a lighter trumpet-blast. That would be the baby elephant showing off its musical talents.

There was no doubt, Bill told himself, that he and Ginny had ended up in the heart of No Man's Land—pure elephant country.

(2)

For the rest of the day the three behaved more like juvenile delinquents than like elephants.

Keeping their activities to the area surrounding the bungalow and caravan, which included a small pool by the bungalow, the two adults and the baby elephant spent some of their time splashing each other with liquid red mud, but what seemed to attract them most were the flower beds. They had a high old time with these. They pulled up the flowers, ate them, pulled up the plants and ate those.

The baby elephant had picked up a flower-pot outside the bungalow, and when Bill, watching from the shelter of the verandah, shouted out: "Put that down," the baby duly obeyed. Dropping the flower-pot to the ground, it devoured the flowers with considerable appetite.

"Well, at any rate, he is obedient," Bill said to Ginny. "When he wants to be, that is."

Bill and Ginny divided the time between the verandah, the caravan and the bungalow, keeping a wary eye on the elephants in case of any danger. Though what they could have done had danger materialised was doubtful. They were pretty well trapped in the vicinity of the bungalow and the caravan.

"I really don't think it's wise of you to venture out," Bill said to Ginny, from behind a hurriedly erected barricade of garden chairs at the entrance to the verandah.

"I don't think it would be wise for you to either," she said. Bill did not require to have his arm twisted to accept her advice.

All the time as they kept a look-out against an attack, they experienced the uncomfortable feeling that they were themselves being watched, that the elephants, even while they were playing, had Bill and Ginny in view out of the corners of their eyes, so to speak. Once, when Ginny handed Bill a plate of beans at a moment when he wasn't expecting it, she nearly made him jump out of his skin. He was convinced that one of the elephants had crept up on him. After various private games, the rules of which were somewhat foreign to Bill and Ginny, they began to feel that the slap-happy trio out there in the flower-beds or splashing in the pool were giving a performance, putting on a show for Bill's and Ginny's benefit. They had to admit that dangerous as they might appear, the trio's cavortings were decidedly amusing.

"They really are quite characters, aren't they?" Bill said.

Ginny gave him a sharp look.

"Characters?" She glanced again at one of the adult elephants who was busy uprooting a flower-bed, roots and all. "So that's what Tom meant," she mused. "He didn't mean that the bungalow had character, he meant that the bungalow had characters."

The audience, including the squirrel and geckos, who had been watching the three elephants with fascination, had been joined by a superb starling.

Despite the moments of extreme apprehension which they suffered, Ginny and Bill could not help realising that the elephants were true characters as Tom Woodson had described them, each with a distinctive personality. Ginny thought it only fair to give them names. The first of the trio—this was the sort of middle one—they decided should be called Kadengi. This was one of the two African words that they knew between them. Funnily enough, neither of them could remember what it meant. But it sounded suitable for an elephant.

The second elephant, who was the biggest, they christened Jasper, after Bill's grandfather. "There's a similarity about the ears," Bill told Ginny.

As for the little one, they couldn't think what to call it, until Bill decided that he really ought to try and make a dash for it, at any rate to the landrover, and bring it nearer the bungalow.

Choosing a moment when he felt certain that the elephants' eyes were no longer on him Bill dodged out of the bungalow, skipped across the verandah, over the barricade, and reached the landrover.

As he was about to call upon "Mr. Mopagee" to oblige as before, he saw, out of the corner of his eye, that the baby elephant was making a bee-line for him. Bill took off back to the bungalow. By now the baby elephant had caught up with him, its trunk outstretched like a clutching hand to haul him back, and Bill began shouting over his shoulder.

"Steady—steady—steady—slowly—slowly," then remembering what he believed was the African for "slowly" he added: "Polé, polé, steady, now steady—"

He reached the verandah and leapt the barricade. Ginny grabbed his hand and hurriedly they dashed back into the bungalow.

After a few moments, Bill and Ginny returned to the verandah and saw the baby elephant standing there looking inside with the greatest curiosity. Then, apparently satisfied with what it saw, it turned away. They plucked up enough courage to come out and urge the baby elephant away from the bungalow.

"Polé, polé—" Bill muttered persuasively, pronouncing it to rhyme with roly-poly. "Slowly, slowly—push off, push off—polé—polé—" which was how the baby elephant became known as Polé-Polé, or, alternatively, Slowly-Slowly.

The baby turned away and trotted off to the two big elephants. Ginny and Bill watched it from the verandah. Bill shook his head.

"We're entirely surrounded," he said. "Cut off from humanity. We could be stuck here for weeks."

"How exciting," Ginny said. Then she added thoughtfully: "I could write a book."

She was smiling dreamily at the prospect of sitting down with writing paper and pencil, scribbling away about her adventures with the elephants. Bill reminded her that it would not turn out to be quite as easy as all that. She would be too busily employed coping with the cooking and housekeeping—not forgetting the three elephants themselves. The right place to write would be in the comfort, quiet and seclusion of their home in Dorking, he told her.

Even so, Ginny did not seem to be all that disturbed by the prospect of being cooped up in the bungalow by Kadengi, Jasper and Slowly-Slowly for the next couple of weeks or so.

Chapter 6

(1)

THEY were watching the three elephants hovering near the trees, and now it seemed that their attention was fixed on Bill and Ginny. Then, Slowly-Slowly and the elephant they had christened Kadengi moved off, while Jasper remained behind, still hovering. Bill pointed this out to Ginny. She thought perhaps is was because Jasper liked the shade. As they watched Jasper, he spread out his ears.

"If only he didn't spread his ears so," Bill said, apprehensively. "It's unnerving."

"He's only waving," Ginny replied. "Just being friendly."

Bill gave a sceptical snort. 'All 5,000 pounds of him."

He was to learn that flapping their ears was, in fact, only a way elephants have for keeping cool. An elephant's ears are criss-crossed with little veins and arteries, and waving them helps to keep the temperature down.

Whatever course of action the trio had been contemplating—if, indeed, they had been thinking of getting up to any tricks at all—Jasper turned away and joined the other two. They appeared to have lost interest in Ginny and Bill, at any rate for the moment. The three of them began eating the flowers again, while Slowly-Slowly and Kadengi played a game. First of all Kadengi nudged the baby, then Jasper nudged Slowly-Slowly, as if they were pretending that the baby was attempting to get away.

Chin sunk on hand, Bill leaned on the verandah wall and sighed heavily. "Quite frankly, I can't think what to do next," he said.

A thought occurred to Ginny. "It's a pity," she said, "that they aren't a bit smaller—"

Bill stared at her. "Why?"

"Like lions—"

"Lions?" Bill said. "Lions—" he said again. "Of course!" Ginny looked at him. His eyes had suddenly lit up with excitement. "That's it."

"That's what?"

He turned to her with animation. "We'll go and see George Adamson—he knows all there is to know about animals. Elephants as well as lions."

"George—?"

"He'll know what to do," Bill said confidently.

"Brilliant," Ginny said.

So that was that. They looked at each other as if the problem were solved there and then. Then Ginny gave a little frown.

"There's just one snag," she said.

"Snag?" Bill looked puzzled. He couldn't see that there was any snag about it.

Bill had acted the role of George Adamson and Ginny had played his wife, Joy, in *Born Free*, the film based on Joy Adamson's famous book about Elsa the lioness. The Adamsons had worked on the film during its production in Africa, and Bill and Ginny had become great friends with them.

George, as Bill and Ginny knew, was now running a camp not far distant, at Mugwongo, in the middle of the Meru Game Reserve, where he had formed a pride of lions with the object of rehabilitating them so that they could live and enjoy a natural life in their wild state. The pride comprised lions which had taken part in *Born Free*, and their cubs, together with other cubs that had been give him.

He had, as Bill said, formerly been a game-warden in that part of East Africa, and would know exactly how to cope with Jasper, Kadengi and Slowly-Slowly.

"Snag?" Bill was asking Ginny. "What snag?"

She nodded in the direction of the elephants. Following her look, Bill noted that they had moved away from the trees towards the landrover. It was apparent that they intended to investigate this brightly striped vehicle, with its tattered canvas hood.

"How do we get to 'Mr. Mopagee'?" asked Ginny.

Bill paused, his mouth slightly open. "Oh, yes," he said slowly. "I see what you mean."

He eyed the three elephants calculatingly. He glanced at them, then at the landrover and then back to the elephants. "They're in a very strategic position," he admitted.

By now the three elephants were circling round "Mr. Mopagee" regarding it with deep interest. In a moment, Slowly-Slowly pushed her trunk out tentatively and pulled on a piece of rope hanging from the landrover. Another rent appeared in the canvas roof.

"We'll have to create a diversion," Bill decided.

Ginny was looking thoughtfully at the trio circling the landrover. "I know," she said suddenly.

"What—?"

"You go round the side of the bungalow," she said, "to attract their attention. Create a diversion. Do anything— start picking flowers."

Bill stared at her uneasily.

"Start picking flowers?" He didn't like the idea at all. "It's a woman's job, really," he said.

A few minutes later, Bill was making his way cautiously from the verandah, not without stumbling over a chair that was in his way. Ginny looked on, her face bright with excitement. Bill still thought that picking flowers was a woman's job, but he reminded himself he was a diversion, and it was his duty to proceed accordingly.

He paused, and then began moving towards the flowering plants. Meanwhile, Ginny was keeping an eye on the elephants. It seemed to her that Slowly-Slowly's attention was shifting from the landrover. But was her husband making the most of the situation? For one thing, from where they were, none of the elephants could see him. She thought it was essential that Bill should reach that part of the flower-beds where the elephants would immediately see him and move towards him, and give up the investigation of possibilities of playful games they could have with the landrover.

"What are you waiting for?" she called out. "They can't see you from where you are."

Bill was, in fact, almost hidden behind a flowering bush in front of the bungalow. He gave a nod in answer to Ginny's observation, then crept towards a tree a few yards beyond the flowering bush. He reached some flower-beds behind which he hid himself momentarily. Then he decided this might be the moment to attract the attention of Slowly-Slowly.

Feverishly he started to pick flowers. He stood up and called out:

"Slowly-Slowly, look!" He held out some flowers which he had pulled up. "Here!"

The baby elephant raised its trunk and began moving in Bill's direction.

Ginny called out encouragingly: "It's coming for you!"

Bill turned towards her sharply, as if to say that he could tell that for himself, he didn't need her advice on that score. Only it wasn't Slowly-Slowly she was referring to, it was Kadengi.

The second largest of the two elephants had begun lumbering towards him, ears stuck out like windmills. It was enough for Bill. He took off like a shot from a gun and landed inside the verandah, almost on his hands and knees. He was still clutching the flowers he had picked. Ginny regarded him tenderly.

"Oh Bill," she said, as she took the flowers from him, "you haven't brought me flowers for ages."

Bill looked at her in dismay. "You're supposed to be sitting in 'Mr. Mopagee'," he said.

His tone was somewhat edgy. After all, he had risked his life . . . Ginny smiled down at him and sniffed the flowers. "Oh, I couldn't go without you."

Bill raised himself to his full height, contriving to roll his eyes heavenwards while at the same time looking down at her with an exasperated expression. It was quite an accomplishment. "But that was the whole idea," he groaned.

Ginny looked at him innocently.

"Oh, I see," she said and she took another sniff at the flowers.

Bill glanced at the elephants and his expression lightened. It seemed to him that they had given up their investigation of the landrover and were going away.

He grabbed Ginny's wrist. "Quick—now's our chance," he said, his voice rising with tension.

Ginny took off like a bird as he dragged her from the verandah. With her clinging to him precariously, they rushed towards the landrover. They jumped inside. Then Bill jumped out to open the bonnet.

"Mr. Mopagee—" he began, then sensed, rather than saw, the elephants behind him.

He spun round on his heels. Jasper, ears wide like sails in a strong wind, was moving purposely towards him. He made as if to move round from the bonnet to the car door and then saw Kadengi approaching, obviously to intecept him.

Quickly Bill changed onto his other foot and sped round the bonnet in an attempt to get into the vehicle from the other side. But by this time Jasper looked as if at any minute he would block Bill's way. And now, coming from the other side, Slowly-Slowly was moving towards him. Her ears were not so big, but they spread out menacingly.

A moment of panic seized Bill, and he slid underneath the landrover. "Mr. Mopagee—" he shouted.

Ginny could see no sign of her husband. She saw the three elephants converging on her. Panic filled her as it had filled Bill and she jiggled the starting-key. "Mr. Mopagee" choked into life and the landrover rattled like a batch of skeletons on a corrugated iron roof.

At the same time, Jasper's trunk searched underneath the vehicle. Black, oily drips were hanging from the sump. Bill covered his face with his arm and wriggled further underneath. Then, from the other side, Kadengi's trunk also investigated the situation under the landrover; and now Slowly-Slowly's trunk lifted up and began to tickle the side of Ginny's face. At the same moment, Kadengi's tusks appeared at the window by the driving-seat.

Ginny gave a scream, let in the clutch and the landrover began to move off. From underneath Bill yelled out, but a bewildered Ginny, who had no idea where he was, put her foot down on the accelerator. She fought desperately with the steering-wheel to avoid hitting the bungalow. As she swung round she head a despairing cry.

"Wait for me!"

Bill was left flat on his back without any protection from the three elephants, and Ginny, hearing his shouts, slowed up.

As it happened, the landrover leaving Bill behind had the effect of putting a stop to the elephants manoeuvring, which gave Bill a chance to scramble to his feet and chase after Ginny.

"Wait for me, wait for me!"

Ginny turned and saw him. She managed to get "Mr. Mopagee" under control, slowed down sufficiently for him to clamber aboard the second time round, and they drove off in a cloud of exhaust-fumes and red dust in the direction of George Adamson's camp.

Chapter 7

(1)

SOME while later, Ginny was pouring tea for Bill and George Adamson, outside his small bungalow near the foot of Mugwongo, a rock hill surrounded on three sides by plain and on the fourth side, swamp, thorn-bushes and palm-trees. George Adamson was of medium height, silver-haired, with a small silvery beard. Almost invariably he smoked a pipe.

"Oh, yes," Bill was saying with elaborate nonchalance, referring to Kadengi, Jasper and Slowly-Slowly, "although they seem quite wild, whenever I show my face, they keep a respectable distance."

Ginny handed him his cup of tea.

She didn't believe that George was taken in for one moment by Bill's effort to sound casual about the elephants.

"You'd never believe it," she said, "but we had to make a run for it."

As she spoke, a lion, followed by a lioness, padded past, to disappear round the corner of the bungalow. Neither she nor Bill took any notice; they were used to George's lions—after all, they had lived with them for almost a year and had come to know and love them, while they were making *Born Free*. That film, from the book, had concerned itself with the trust and love that can be created between human beings and lions. No part of what was, after all, an unusual relationship had been faked.

George's camp was enclosed with strong link-mesh netting, nailed to six-foot high poles. It was divided into an enclosure for George's ancient land-rover, and the camp compound where there were tents and the small bungalow for George and his assistants.

The eleven lions that formed George's pride lived outside, enjoying a free and natural life; right from the start, the very day George had set up the camp, they made free of the entire place, coming and going as they pleased. Even at night, some of them often didn't bother to return to their enclosure, but slept on the top of George's landrover.

"It was quite nerve-wracking," Ginny was continuing; she was relating the escape she and Bill had made from the elephants.

Bill sipped at his cup of tea. Now he glanced up, his manner still elaborately casual.

"Oh, you do exaggerate sometimes," he said to Ginny. He turned to George. "Actually, George, I was pottering about the garden picking flowers for Ginny."

Ginny's eyes were raised in disbelief, but Bill went on. "When suddenly we decided to visit you."

George took the cup of tea Ginny had poured for him. As he sipped it, he said over the rim of the cup: "Was it a big herd?"

Bill paused for a moment. "A crowd would be more accurate."

"Really, Bill," Ginny protested. She turned to George. "There were three. Two big ones and a little one."

"That's what I said," Bill said, unabashed. "Three's a crowd—"

Ginny waved a teaspoon at him to keep quiet, while she went on: "And the young one was absolutely adorable."

George put his cup down and said to her: "Most unusual for young elephants to leave the herd. Are they doing much damage?"

"Six potted plants—" Ginny began, and Bill interrupted her.

"And a creeper," he said.

George listened carefully to everything they could tell him about these three uninvited guests. At the end, he nodded understandingly. "I should go and see Charles Matiso, the gamewarden of your area," he said. "He's your man."

After tea, Bill and Ginny strolled round the area to say hello to the lions. There was Girl, who had played Elsa in the film; her brother, Boy—he had played the goat-stealing lion—who had accidentally broken Ginny's leg during rehearsals; and there was Ugas, who was one-eyed now as the result of an encounter, it was believed, with a spitting cobra, and who had enacted the role of the man-eater in *Born Free*. There were also four young lions born

An Elephant Called 'Slowly'
Meets Ginny and Bill Travers

On their arrival in Nairobi, Ginny and Bill pick up the keys to their rented landrover and set out to find Tom Woodson's bungalow, deep in a remote part of Kenya. It's an embarrassing moment for Ginny when she tries to wipe the windscreen glass—and finds there isn't any!

After the first night in their new home Bill and Ginny discover that they have been invaded by three playful elephants. They look on in amazement as two of them, mother and baby, investigate the unusual vehicle, "Mr. Mopagee," in the hope of finding something edible.

George Adamson and one of the lions from Born Free are on hand to greet Ginny and Bill when they arrive at his compound. The rest of the pride wanders about freely.

"Girl," another old friend from Born Free days, welcomes the Travers in her own way. Like a contented kitten she lies at Ginny's feet to have her head scratched.

Back at the bungalow, Bill and Ginny realize they have been "adopted" and learn to appreciate their unique situation. Who else has an elephant in the backyard?

"What do you do when you are approached by a rhinoceros?" Ginny asked.

"I think we ought to stand perfectly still," Bill answered, but he didn't sound too sure.

Making friends with a rhino is not so hard after all.

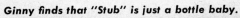
Ginny finds that "Stub" is just a bottle baby.

"Slowly-Slowly" leads the way on an afternoon ramble.

It's a strange feeling walking with an elephant, Ginny thought to herself. Suddenly you feel cut down to size.

The baby elephant shows her appreciation for all the trouble Bill took to make a nice mud wallow for her.

With her inquisitive trunk "Slowly" tries to find out what goodies the Travers have brought for her this time.

Perhaps intending to do some gardening, "Slowly" retrieves a shovel her mother had found near the bungalow.

"Eleanor" ambles over to the bath house where Bill is happily scrubbing away, unaware that he is about to receive a shower he hadn't counted on.

When the time comes to say good-bye, Ginny and Bill wonder how their new friends will get along without them.

The Travers make certain that there is a herd of elephants living in the wild nearby, so that "Eleanor," "Kadengi," and "Slowly-Slowly" will find friends and be safe from hunters.

As a farewell gift to the friendly rhinos at Charles Matiso's camp, Ginny and Bill offer lollipops. Rudi, finds the stick especially tasty.

"Eleanor" does her best to help Bill get the landrover in shape for the return trip to Nairobi, causing Bill to give up entirely.

With their adopted family gone, the friendly trio head back into the bush.

in captivity, whom George was training to live the free and natural life to which they belonged—Susua, a male, and Suki, Sally and Shaitani.

It was George who four years ago, now, had played such an important part in showing Bill and Ginny how to live with lions, how to understand and be friends with them, during the filming. His gentle manner and approving chuckle had given them tremendous encouragment, without which they could never have met the special demands that the roles of Joy and George Adamson had made upon them.

After all, they had never had friends before like Boy, Girl, and Ugas, and the other lions in the film—so amazingly affectionate, such powerful personalities. Now the three lions came and rubbed their heads against them, in the way lions greet each other in the pride. They were remembered with the same old affection, with low, soft lion calls. Seeing the lions again, Bill and Ginny recalled the alarms, and hazards they had encountered—but, most of all, they remembered their unusual and wonderful comradeship shared during the endless months of training and filming. They grew to understand the lions—and, they believed, the lions came to understand a little about them in return.

They recalled the walks with George and the lions in the dew-fresh mornings; the games they played together to establish better contacts—football, stalking—and the lunch-time picnics. There was one young lioness named Henrietta, who adored sardines—although usually the others didn't care much for "civilised" foods, such as chicken or ham. Bill and Ginny would always be grateful to George and the lions, from who they had learned so much.

But it was time for them to return to the matter

of the three elephants, to call upon Charles Matiso.
They would be back, of course. George was sure
of that, as he waved them off. They would be back.

(2)

On their way to Charles Matiso's home, they saw
a herd of impala in the distance. They drew nearer,
and Bill stopped the landrover.

Ginny stared at the breath-taking sight of these
beautiful animals; they were a sleek, reddish-brown
in colour, with large, limpid brown eyes. Bill
noticed a single impala vigorously rubbing its lyre-
shaped horns in the grass, burying the points and
uprooting huge tufts which it flung into the air.

"They're so graceful," Ginny was saying, and
then broke off as she too watched the male impala,
"except for that big show-off—"

"Well," Bill pointed out, "he's got a lot to brag
about."

Ginny looked at him questioningly.

"Haven't you noticed," he said, "the rest of the
herd are all females, his harem. It's a marvellous
life—just think of it darling, fifty—or sixty."

He broke off and indicated another group of
female impala which had come into sight.

"What's happened to the rest of the males?" Ginny asked.

"He's driven them away. They are probably
somewhere nearby waiting their chance." He
shifted his gaze and pointed to a small group of
male impala. Ginny followed his glance.

"Don't get much of a look-in, do they?"

"Not much," Bill agreed. He added: "That is,
until some predator—might be a leopard—comes
along and scatters the herd, leaving the females
unprotected."

Ginny looked at him questioningly again. "What then?"

"Every man for himself," Bill answered her.

She noticed that the impala constantly stamped their feet and twitched themselves, to shake the flies off their legs; impala are meticulously clean.

Slowly, so as not to disturb them, Bill drove on a little further and then Ginny caught sight of a lone female impala in the grass by the edge of some trees. She appeared nervous, but made no attempt to move. Ginny pointed her out to Bill, who cut the engine. Something was wrong. He saw a movement, and from behind the impala's hind legs there appeared her baby. It was newly born.

Its mother was beside it, licking it gently, cleaning up the after-birth, as the baby made a tremendous effort to stand up.

"Oh, look," Ginny whispered. "It's tiny."

"I wonder what they will call it?" Bill said.

Ginny smiled. "Bambi, I suppose," she said. 'It's inevitable, isn't it?"

The new-born impala was still wet, and still unable to stand. It was then that Bill detected a flicker of leaves in a tree nearby. Ginny was asking him why the mother impala wasn't resting. "She should be—and the baby—"

The mother looked up, her nostrils twitching. She began licking the baby as if urging it to get to its feet. The baby tried; it seemed to understand the sudden urgency in its mother's attentions, who now moved so that her teats were nearer the baby's head. By instinct, the tiny creature exerted all its strength and tried to reach up. It couldn't quite manage it, but the effort did almost get it to its feet.

Bill agreed with Ginny that mother and baby should be resting—he hadn't taken his eyes off the movement he had seen in the tree. Ginny caught the tension in his attitude.

"What is it?" she said.

"There's something moving." Ginny followed the direction in which he was looking. "Over there," Bill said.

They could both see the leopard now as it tensed itself along the branch of the tree. Ginny shuddered and prayed that it had not seen the mother with her new-born baby.

Leopards habitually hunted by leaping on their prey from a tree, where they lay concealed—their spotted coats blending suitably against the dappled sunlight of leaves and branches; and their lofty position enabling them to range the area and spot likely victims. In less remote areas they lie hidden all day, hunting only at night. They often kept a "larder" of food, consisting of their victims, high in a thorn tree, where jackals or hyenas couldn't reach. For some reason, vultures wouldn't attempt to steal the meat kept this way, though they could be seen hanging about in neighbouring trees, ready to pounce when any meat fell to the ground. A leopard could carry quite large animals into its tree-top "larder." But its favourite food were baboons, or animals of the size of gazelles or impala.

The baby impala had managed to scramble to its feet.

It lurched against its mother unsteadily. Bill and Ginny divided their attention between it and its mother and the leopard still crouching along the branch of the tree. Bill wasn't sure that the leopard had actually seen the mother and baby yet; but he felt certain it would have scented the birth and the strong smells consequent upon it. The mother had moved off a little, alert, and anxious for the baby to go to her so that she could lead it to the safety of a clump of trees a few yards distant.

The way she was sniffing at the air, it was obvious now that she had got the leopard's scent.

Ginny glanced to where the leopard was watching them. It was moving down the branch, it seemed to her that it was coiled like some terrific spring ready to leap upon its prey. She whispered to Bill that he must do something—shout or drive the landrover at the leopard, anything in an effort to scare it off, and prevent it attacking the mother and baby. Bill shook his head. Any move they made, he replied, might scare the leopard, but might also precipitate it to leap on its kill and make off with it.

"I wish Bambi would just go," she prayed, "run away. Before . . ."

Her voice trailed away. The baby was too weak yet to move with any speed, but it had started to follow the mother, staggering and falling, then struggling to get up again. That was always the danger with a new-born impala, the first half-hour of life is precarious for any animal born in the wild.

Ginny's eyes were now fixed upon the leopard moving more and more remorselessly along the branch, its attention fixed with unwinking intentness upon the baby and its mother. It seemed obvious to Ginny that it was only a matter of seconds before the leopard would leap to destroy them.

Bill saw that the baby impala was trying to feed from its mother, but as soon as it found her teats she moved on, continuing to persuade it to follow her to safety.

The leopard still moved forward to a position which would give it the best chance to pounce on its prey. The mother impala reached the edge of the undergrowth and the baby, staggering, ran after her.

The palms of Ginny's hands were wet with perspiration and her fingernails dug into them, though she didn't realize the pain of it. Now the leopard paused. At the same moment the mother began edging itself more and more into the clump of trees, the baby following her. Now the pair of them had vanished into the trees' dark, green depths.

Bill and Ginny could hear no sound as the impala moved through the leaves, receding into safer distance. They turned and saw that the leopard had disappeared. There was a stir in the parchment grass beneath the branch of the tree, and then stillness.

Ginny and Bill looked at each other. Bill sat down and let in the clutch as Ginny moved beside him as if for protection.

"I suppose," she said, very quietly, "we won't ever know if she got away safely?"

Bill shook his head, put his foot on the accelerator and they drove off.

Chapter 8

(1)

A SHORT while later found them at the main entrance gates of the reserve, beyond which were Charles Matiso's headquarters. They comprised a bungalow and other buildings in the middle of a dusty road with the great mountains in the background. Informed by one of the African parkrangers that Matiso himself was down by the river, Ginny and Bill proceeded along the sandy track through bush country, until they halted near the river-bank.

On the way to Chales Matiso, "Mr. Mopagee" had not been on his best form. Apart from having hiccoughs, and indulging in bursts of back-firing, large jets of steam shot up from his bonnet at irregular intervals. Ginny and Bill decided that "Mr. Mopagee" deserved a rest, he was extremely hot, so they got out of the landrover and made their way on foot towards the river, keeping an eye open for the gamewarden. It was a beautiful day, the purple mountains and the great plains stretching serenely as far as the eye could see.

Suddenly Ginny touched Bill's arm.

"What do you do when you see two rhinos?" she asked.

Bill had paused as she had done. "Same as you do when you see one," he said.

"What's that?"

Bill was about to say he would run like mad, when he saw the two rhinos to which Ginny had been referring appear over the river-bank. He and Ginny froze like blocks of ice. After a few moments, she said to him in a nervous whisper: "Do you think they'd notice if we walked quietly away?"

He hesitated, then he said: "I think we ought to stand perfectly still." The two rhinos were closing in on them. Bill said, without a great deal of conviction in his voice, "They probably haven't seen us. They are very shortsighted."

"I wish I was," Ginny said.

Both of them found themselves taking a step or two back. The two rhinos continued coming towards them. Ginny glanced at Bill, as if expecting him to produce some inspiration which would get them out of the jam they were in. He seemed to have nothing to say.

All he appeared capable of doing was glancing rather wildly from right to left.

"I personally think we should make a run for 'Mr. Mopagee'," Ginny said.

Bill threw a hasty glance over his shoulder. "Mr. Mopagee" which he had thought was a couple of hundred yards away, now seemed to have receded to the horizon. A glance back at the two rhinos showed that they had moved more and more between the landrover and themselves. He shook his head.

"What shall we do?" Ginny's tone sounded distinctly discouraged.

"If they charge—" Bill began, whereupon Ginny uttered a cry of dismay. "If they charge—" Bill began again, and Ginny looked at him expectantly. "Yes—?"

"We're in a very tricky position," Bill said, somewhat lamely.

Ginny frowned at him with heightened indignation. She had left it to him to take command of the situation, and surely he should be able to think up something more enterprising than that? The two rhinos were still coming towards them. They could hear their heavy breathing, and see their small, beady eyes fixed on them. Then, at that moment, Ginny and Bill heard a noise behind them. They swung round. It was a safari truck approaching.

The rhinos had broken into an ungainly trot. But it was the new arrival and not themselves, who had attracted their attention; as the safari truck drew to a halt, Charles Matiso got out. An African guard also got out of the truck on the other side. Bill touched Ginny's arm and she turned round as Matiso came forward.

"Glad to see you," the African gamewarden said.

"I heard you were here." He was a wiry, alert personality, with a warm smile on his face.

"You're glad to see us?" Ginny echoed fervently. "You don't know how glad we are to see you."

Bill couldn't help noticing that Charles Matiso was unconcerned at what appeared to be the rhinos' dangerous advance. Though they had slowed down, they were still coming forward.

"Do you happen to have noticed what's coming up on our starboard side?" he said. He quite surprised himself that he managed to sound so nonchalant.

Matiso looked past him and Ginny. "You mean the two rhinos?"

"Yes," Bill said. He was edging himself and Ginny closer to the safari truck which had arrived so opportunely. "Do you mind if we come aboard?"

Matiso's brown face was creased in a wider smile.

"Don't worry about them," he said, "they're very friendly—just a couple of orphans. Just stand still, that's the best way."

Bill gaped at him for a moment, then he turned to Ginny.

"There, I told you," he said, the confident smugness returning to his voice. "Just stand still."

"You didn't know they were pets," she replied.

"I suspected it."

"Liar."

The two rhinos had halted a few yards away, and started to feed on a bush. Matiso told Bill and Ginny that they were well-known characters, and perfectly friendly. One of them, named Rufus, while still young had been found abandoned several years before and Matiso had carefully brought him up.

Rufus had responded so well to kindness that now he was allowed to wander about, free to come and go as he wished. It was a few years later, Matiso continued, that Rufus had come home one day with a friend, an almost fully grown rhino which had never had any contact with human beings.

By now Bill and Ginny were both fondling the rhinos, stroking their heads, scratching them behind the ears. The rhinos were uttering small, high-pitched squeaks of pleasure, an unexpectedly tiny sound from such huge animals. Matiso went on to explain that Rudy, as the second rhino was named, had also responded to kindness—"as most animals do," Bill said, and Ginny nodded. Matiso agreed and he went on to explain that neither of these pre-historic-looking creatures, so often believed to be highly dangerous, had ever found it necessary to throw its weight about.

"And they could have," Bill said, with a glance at the enormous creature who was allowing Ginny to fondle it. There was all of 3,000 pounds of it.

"Why not come up to my house," Matiso said. "I have another one there."

"Bigger?" Bill queried.

Matiso laughed, "No, not bigger, but he has a rhino-sized thirst."

He explained that it was a baby rhino that was being fed from the bottle.

(2)

A little while later, Bill watched while Ginny fed the baby rhino which had been introduced to them as Stub. He was called that because of his size and shape. He was by far the smallest of the three and still really a baby, his little horns no more than triangular projections on his long brow. Pint-sized he may have been in the rhino world, but he had the thirst of a racing-car.

Despite attempts to eradicate the supersition that rhinos' horns possess mysterious aphrodisiac properties, they are still sought in some Asiatic countries as an essential ingredient in so-called love potions. For this reason rhinos are in danger of being slaughtered out of existence by poachers. The rhinos' horns, of which there are normally two, are, in fact, peculiar amongst mammals. The horn is less of a bony composition than is a cow's for example, or an elephant's tusk; it is of a more hairy substance. It lacks a core of bone, and is not fused to the skull, but merely attached to the skin.

A female rhino, living in the Amboseli National Reserve, famous for the length of one of her horns, which grew to an estimated fifty-four inches, was named Gertie. It was often broken off, but always grew again. Another rhino living in Amboseli, named Gladys, also possessed a pair of elongated horns which were always being broken off. Gladys was killed by poachers. Poachers and hunters with, not unnaturally, a vested interest in publicising the ferocity of their victims, have continued to describe rhinos as vicious-tempered and ferocious, but, in fact, they are just as inclined to retreat as to attack when provoked.

A rhino is especially short-sighted and lives in constant fear of an enemy creeping up on it, unseen. This explains why it may attack at the slightest sound in its immediate vicinity. But as Ginny and Bill were quickly discovering, when befriended by humans rhino can be extremely gentle.

Even a fully grown animal is easily tamed, given affection and a friendly atmosphere.

Stub, who was enjoying his third bottle which Ginny was holding for him, had been found after a forest fire. His mother had been burnt to death. The experience gained in rearing Rufus, Matiso said, had proved invaluable in keeping Stub alive. After the first few difficult months he gained strength and weight rapidly. He got on well with Rufus and Rudy, and was free, like them, to go where and when he pleased. But he seldom wandered out of earshot. In case, Ginny suggested, as she continued to feed him, there was a further clink of bottles.

Ginny moved away from him, trying to remove the empty bottle, and Stub followed her, still sucking at it tenaciously.

"We're not really troubled by rhinos," Ginny explained at Matiso. "Elephants are our problem."

"The biggest of them," Bill said, "we've called Jasper, after my grandfather."

Matiso eyed him curiously. "The biggest?" he said. "It is impossible—Jasper is a girl." Bill and Ginny exchanged surprised looks.

Charles Matiso seemed to know all about the three particular elephants. He caught Bill's and Ginny's expressions of surprise and told them he had come across the happy wanderers already. The trio had made themselves quite well known in the neighbourhood. And Tom Woodson had reported their presence to the gamewarden.

"Oh," Bill said, "then we'll have to call her Eleanor, after my grandfather's wife." There were occasions when Bill conveyed the distinct impression that he possessed a somewhat one-track mind.

"That's your grandmother, isn't it?" Ginny said. Bill nodded, and she turned to Matiso.

"Well, they're round the house all the time. We are completely surrounded."

Matiso regarded her and Bill for a moment. It looked to him, he said, as if the elephants had adopted them. Ginny asked what he meant by that. Matiso replied that it was very logical, because the three of them were orphans, too.

Ginny thought about it for a moment. "We're not orphans," she said.

"No, but they don't know that," Matiso said patiently, as if the explanation was transparently clear, "do they?"

Chapter 9

(1)

BACK at Tom Woodson's bungalow, and encouraged by what they had learned from Charles Matiso, Bill and Giny started at once to follow his example. The quickest way to an elephant's heart was obviously through its stomach, and Bill and Ginny fed Kadengi, Eleanor (as Jasper was now renamed) and Slowly-Slowly with sweet potato tops and oranges.

Then Bill thought that perhaps a good way to help them forge their friendship with the three elephants was to observe others—there being plenty of elephants in the vicinity—to see what sort of food they enjoyed most, and their general behaviour. Together with Ginny, he set off in the landrover next day, to find the nearest herd.

As they drove through the trees and the undergrowth they passed some tiny antelope, Dikdik, with long noses which they wiggled from side to side and a group of other very beautiful species of deer, Gerenuk, sometimes called giraffe-necked deer, because of their extremely long necks. With their large ears on the alert, the Gerenuk watched the landrover go past.

Bill and Ginny drove along a dusty red track

through bush country, until they saw elephant droppings on the road. They turned off and followed the signs through the dried-up undergrowth. Suddenly, Bill slammed on the brakes and they came to a stop. There, ahead of them, was a herd of elephants. Short-sighted though they were, the herd quickly caught their scent and began careering around, trumpeting loudly, with ears outspread, their attention directed toward Bill and Ginny in the landrover.

Bill became quite certain that they were preparing to charge, and he reversed through the bushes back on the landrover's tracks. One big bull elephant pursued them for a short distance, trumpeting defiantly.

"They weren't pleased to see us," Ginny gasped.

"I think we startled them a little," Bill replied.

Ginny's heart was pounding madly.

"*We* startled *them*?" she said.

They had reached a rough track through green trees and bushes, and came out to an open space. Ahead they saw a herd of buffalo, white egrets flapping about them like giant snowflakes. Bill realized that he should have known that when approaching the elephants, the most important thing to do was to keep down wind.

They might have poor eyesight, he said to Ginny, but he should have remembered that they possessed a jolly good sense of smell.

"You just forgot, darling," she comforted him.

Disturbed by the approach of the landrover the egrets left the backs of the buffalo on which they were perched and flew around in a sort of snowstorm. The buffalo seemed not to mind the presence of strangers, and Bill reminded Ginny, crouching down in the landrover, that they seldom charged when they were in a herd. She was not quite convinced that he was sure his information was one hundred per cent correct.

"Anyway," he said optimistically, "they're busy. Yes," he went on, "they're stuffing themselves and at the same time providing a meal for the birds."

Ginny looked at him questioningly.

"Their hooves disturb the thick matted grass where all the insects hide," he explained. "This starts the insects hopping around like mad, and that's what the egrets feed on, and that's why they too are hopping around like mad."

"The egrets depend on the buffalo, then?" Ginny said.

Bill said: "To some extent."

"Like you depend on me?"

Bill regarded her lovingly and admitted, grudgingly, "Yes, darling, to some extent."

They drove further along the track through green bush. And then, ahead of them in the distance, they saw another herd of elephants.

"Are they down wind this time?" Ginny asked.

"I think so," Bill said slowly. He licked his finger and held it up to the light breeze, and seemed satisfied his calculation was right.

They watched the elephants stripping the bark off an uprooted yellow fever tree. To Ginny, the name of the trees seemed sinister, but Bill explained that for elephants the bark of the trees was an extremely delectable food. "Absolutely delicious."

"In salads?" Ginny asked.

Bill ignored the question, stopped the landrover, and he and his wife got out.

They were not too near the elephants, who, anyway, looked as if they were going to be busy for a while, and there were some more yellow fever trees close at hand. Ginny and Bill started to peel off some of the bark following the example set by the herd. Ginny thought that this should solve the food problem of their new-found friends back at the bungalow.

But although the elephants managed easily enough, removing the bark was not so simple as it looked. Bill and Ginny found that stripping off two or three lengths of the bark was enormously hard work. Obviously it would be an impossible job to carry off enough to feed Kadengi, Eleanor and Slowly-Slowly. Bill reckoned that if they worked hard all day he and Ginny would collect no more than one good mouthful of the stuff for each elephant.

They gave up and watched the elephants in the near distance as they continued feeding off the trees. The yellow fever trees were especially beautiful. It seemed to Bill that the elephants must be mad smashing down lovely nourishing trees like that.

It was Ginny who offered an explanation for the destruction of the trees by the elephants.

"You see, from the point of view of conservation, all the tons of water a particular tree must suck up each day, and which has been destroyed by the elephants, can now be used to grow lots and lots of nice, new healthy grass. Grass," she continued, "is the main part of elephants' diet and will support twice as many elephants as the trees."

Bill frowned at her. "But do you mean to tell me that the elephants know this—that grass will grow to replace the trees they tear down?"

"Who knows what an elephant knows?"

"And who knows what you know?" Bill said, not unimpressed by the information she had given.

Then Ginny explained to him that she had learned it from Charles Matiso.

Not far off, in a small clearing, they saw a baby elephant lying in the grass and it occurred to Ginny that she hadn't seen an elephant lying down before. Bill agreed that when they are fully grown you seldom see them lying down.

"Unless," he added bitterly, "they have been shot."

Ginny shuddered. They were so beautiful, she thought, who would want to kill them?

But she knew the answer to that question. Poachers—for ivory—and hunters—for fun.

She saw that the baby elephant, after considerable rocking and rolling from side to side, had at last managed to clamber to its feet, although with a considerable amount of difficulty. It looked somewhat like Slowly-Slowly she thought, but smaller.

But Bill thought it was much younger. Ginny wondered how old Slowly-Slowly was, and Bill thought it must be aged at least four years. This seemed much too old, Ginny felt, but Bill told her it must be aged over three years, since elephants suckle their young for the first three years—which struck Ginny as being quite an agonizingly long time.

She and Bill watched a big bull elephant stretch up its trunk to break off some tender shoots from a tree, as, not to be outdone when it came to passing on information such as Ginny had just been imparting, Bill went on to say that an elephant's trunk had something like 4,000 muscles in it. Ginny was suitably impressed though she did wonder if perhaps Bill had also been having a chat with Charles Matiso. As she watched the elephants eating the grass and picking up twigs it seemed to her that they used their trunks for everything. They were definitely all-purpose; she even saw one elephant scratching its ear with its trunk; another was using it like a periscope to sniff out any possible threat of danger; while yet another was using her trunk like a mother's hand to chastise an erring child.

Deciding they had obtained all the knowledge they could at that moment concerning the eating habits of elephants, Bill and Ginny turned back as inconspicuously as they could in "Mr. Mopagee" to the bungalow.

(2)

On the way they came across a group of impala and a little further on some gazelles. They paused to watch the graceful creatures, with their pale fawn and white coats and distinctive charcoal marks along each side. They were named Thomson's Gazelle, also known as Tommys. Ginny was amused at the way they wagged their tails—not like a dog, from side to side, but flicked nervously round and round.

"It must be because they're so happy," Ginny said. They looked very happy creatures, she thought.

"More likely to keep the flies away," Bill said.

He and Ginny pushed on. A few hundred yards further, they came to some trees where two young cheetahs were chasing each other around a fallen tree-trunk. Under and over it, they were playing a wonderful game; and watching their beautifully co-ordinated movements in the sun-bleached grass, it occurred to Bill what a tragedy it was that although they didn't know it, those cheetahs were facing extinction.

"If they were not made into fur coats," he said to Ginny, "they would die out soon anyway, because they have nowhere to live. Human beings are gradually taking all their land away from them."

Victims of the population explosion, Ginny could not help thinking.

Now another larger cheetah with a smoother, silkier coat, had come to join the other two. Their mother? Ginny wondered. Suddenly it seemed to Bill and Ginny watching them that the two cheetahs had stopped playing. They had become tense; they had lost interest in their game. Bill and Ginny followed the direction in which they thought the cheetahs were looking and saw the mongoose. Was that, Ginny wondered, what had attracted their attention? But it seemed to her it would be unusual. Even as the thought occurred to her, she saw the mongoose disappear down a hole.

"No, it wasn't the mongoose," Bill said to her, interpreting her thoughts. "It's the Thomson's gazelle.

He pointed out a group of three gazelles and Ginny saw the large cheetah move away from the other two and begin stalking the Tommys. As she watched two of them took off, leaving only the third gazelle. It stood there, lonely and forlorn. Bill touched her arm and pointed out a second cheetah moving in the single gazelle's direction.

Suddenly it realised that danger was imminent. It sprang into action, racing away. But the first cheetah, followed by the second, raced after it.

The Tommy ran, zig-zagging, weaving from side to side. Not because it was intelligent enough to think that it might escape its pursuer in this way but because of the arrangement of its eyes. They are situated on the side of its head and it was turning from side to side in order to get a better view of the cheetah chasing it. It seemed to Bill the frantic gazelle would have moved faster if it had run straight on and not swerved so often to look back.

As for the cheetah, once it sights its victim, its superior speed—bursts of sixty miles an hour is the speed it has been clocked in at, over a short distance—usually enables it to win the race.

This time the race was short; the gazelle had no chance. One moment thirty yards separated it from its pursuer, then the cheetah put in an electrifying burst and soon it and the Tommy were enveloped in a cloud of dust. In no time at all the second cheetah had moved in and both were feeding off the victim. The third, bigger cheetah, which Ginny took to be their mother, moved off, leaving them to their kill.

Ginny had been watching with fascinated horror. "I hoped it would get away," she said quietly. "It ran so fast."

Bill shook his head. "Not as fast as the cheetah," he said. "No animal is."

While the two cheetahs were feeding off the gazelle, partly concealed in the grass, the third one was suddenly aware of the presence of Ginny and Bill and he stared in their direction with a long, unblinking stare. It was strange the way they stared at one, just like a cat, Ginny thought, although she knew they were more like a dog really. At least they were a mixture of dog and cat.

Cheetahs have never been known to attack a man and are, in fact, timid; they can be fairly easily tamed and have a long history of association with man, particularly for hunting purposes. In parts of Asia, the cheetah has been trained for thousands of years to hunt antelope. As Bill had said, it is sensitive to environmental changes brought about by man's encroachment upon the wild places. Cheetah cubs seem to be especially vulnerable to disease, and this is an added hazard which could mean the cheetah's extinction.

Bill and Ginny drove on and presently, amongst some trees, they came upon another group of elephants. They too were feeding on the leaves of the trees and on the grass around. One of the elephants had directed his attention to a tree with long, spiky thorns about two inches long, which are used by natives as needles.

"You'd think," Ginny said, "that it would stick in its cheeks." She found it difficult to believe that these huge animals could keep alive just on grass and thorns. Some of them, she knew, must weigh over 10,000 pounds. Bill explained that after all, the elephants were at it all day. They were eating continually.

"Just one long gargantuan gobble," was how he put it.

"You mean," Ginny replied, "a mammoth munch."

As she watched the elephant deal satisfactorily with the thorns, she began to understand that to support such a great bulk of flesh and bone on what was really a poor diet, elephants need to eat all the time. She recalled something else that Charles Matiso had told her.

If Slowly-Slowly survived everything else, the gamewarden had said, she would ultimately die of starvation anyway.

Elephants' size and monumentally ancient appearance have inspired many tales and legends, especially about the age to which they live. But it is thought that their life-span is sixty years at most. An elephant's natural length of life is, like all mammals', decided by its teeth—once they have gone, and it cannot eat, chew its food, it must die. An elephant's teeth number only four at a time:

one upper and one lower on each side of its jaw, and as these are worn out and shed, others take their place. It is said that there are six sets of these four teeth, and when the last set has gone, then the elephant is doomed. It usally exists for as long as it can on soft water vegetation—and it often dies in the water, which would explain why dead elephants' bones are rarely found on land.

Chapter 10

(1)

AT any rate, they had learned quite a lot from their observation of elephants' feeding habits in the wild, and when they got back to the bungalow they found they were quickly able to attract Slowly-Slowly, and Eleanor and Kadengi, with various leaves and acacia twigs that they set about collecting.

After two or three days it became evident to Bill and Ginny that the elephants had come to the conclusion that they were on to a good thing. They were having their meals handpicked for them. They were always round the bungalow, anticipating being fed and petted. There was no doubt about it, the elephants, in particular Slowly-Slowly, had come to stay. They became increasingly friendly; in particular they enjoyed having their trunks rubbed. Slowly-Slowly spent almost her entire time around the bungalow and the garden, or rather what was left of the garden. She was always hoping that Ginny and Bill would play yet another of her favourite games, "Hunt the orange." Ginny thought she was very intelligent. She played only those games at which she was eventually bound to win.

It was then that Slowly-Slowly found a small pool by the bungalow. It was the size of a small fish-pond, and the spectacle of Slowly-Slowly trying to fit her thousand or so pounds of solid flesh into it decided Ginny that what she ought to have was a large enough pool in which she could wallow. Bill was fully convinced that the pool should remain as it was, for the purpose for which it was built—he visualized a lot of blood, sweat and tears being spilt by him in the project. Ginny was equally insistent that it could be enlarged and filled with sufficient mud to provide the kind of thing which Slowly-Slowly would enjoy.

To illustrate what she meant, she persuaded Bill to drive her in "Mr. Mopagee" to where a herd of elephants had found a large pool which they had converted into a mud-bath. It was obvious, Ginny argued firmly, that this was the sort of thing which Slowly-Slowly would enjoy enormously.

Observing the elephants mudlarking, Bill protested that Slowly-Slowly would only learn to pick up filthy habits, but Ginny insisted that it was quite necessary. Bill couldn't understand what was so necessary about it. After all, it wouldn't help Slowly-Slowly's complexion. Ginny proceeded to point out that it was a protection against dudus and tsetse flies.

Bill failed to see how an elephant with a hide as —(he couldn't think of a more suitable simile)—as an elephant's needed any protection against insects, however venomous they might be. Ginny explained to him patiently that Slowly-Slowly's bloodvessels were very close to the surface and that they were vulnerable in that way to stings.

Despite his loud protests that he wasn't really a wallowing-hole maker, but was only a temporary caretaker in Tom Woodson's absence, Bill finally gave in. Fortunately, Bill discovered there was a laid-on water supply. He set about finding the mud with which he could enlarge the pool near the bungalow, converting it into a wallow of a size suitable for Slowly-Slowly.

Bill filled the back of the landrover with red sand more times than he cared to remember and transported it back to the pool outside the bungalow and shovelled it in, making a very satisfactory wallow.

It was hard work but good for his waistline, Ginny consoled him. Stripped to the waist, Bill shovelled away, and at last the fish-pool was converted into a splendidly soggy mass.

Slowly-Slowly, who had been observing the whole operation from a suitable distance, duly approached. Trying to appear as casual as they could in what was really quite a tense situation, Bill and Ginny watched her. Slowly-Slowly reached the edge of the wallow, her trunk extended over the mud. Raising it, she let out a hollow rumble and still with her trunk in the air, she made off. Nothing that Bill or Ginny could do could persuade her to return—not even the offer of sweet potato tops.

Bill was utterly downcast by Slowly-Slowly's rejection of all that he had done for her, as well as mystified. Ginny could only continue to say, over and over again, that something was wrong, which Bill didn't find very constructive and in fact thought it became slightly irritating. Matters weren't improved when later that afternoon Eleanor and Kadengi ambled along to view Bill's handiwork, and reacted to it in precisely the same manner, turning their trunks up at the lovely, rich, muddy mess and emitting noises which Ginny and Bill could only conclude indicated their disgust. They beat a hasty retreat.

It occurred to Ginny, and she put it to Bill, who felt compelled to acquiesce, that they needed to learn more about what went to making a wallow suitable for elephants.

Ginny felt that they could put in more research by observing some elephants nearby wallowing in a small lake by the river, and off she went with Bill in the landrover.

On the way along the sandy road, through bush country, they passed pink and white flamingos, a picture of enchanting beauty, by the edge of the lake. They disturbed a flock of white birds which flew around in the sky.

"Oh, look," Ginny cried. "Storks. Well, at last, I'll be able to tell the children where they came from—"

She giggled, and Bill gave her an old-fashioned look. As he did so he thought he detected a certain nervous tension which accounted for her little joke, and he realised that she must be suffering a slight strain as a result of the tension and disappointment over the way Slowly-Slowly had rejected her wallow.

"Except for one thing," he said, letting her down as gently as possible.

"What—?"

"They're pelicans."

She glanced up at the white birds above, then gave a shrug of her shoulders. "What difference does it make? You don't really think the children believe all that nonsense—do you?"

She marched ahead, leaving Bill to follow her, muttering to himself something to the effect that one couldn't win—and then, there it was, the herd of elephants Ginny wanted to see. They were taking a marvellous mud-bath in a large depression.

Ginny and Bill watched as the elephants swayed back and forwards in the mud, almost as if they were waltzing to music. There was one baby elephant leaning against a tree-trunk and rhythmically scratching itself with obvious pleasure. A full-grown bull was scratching its stomach on the stump of a tree. Then another elephant began throwing mud over itself, and one flopped down and rolled over and over.

Bill wondered if elephants took mud-baths not only to alleviate the irritation of skin parasites, and to cause them to fall off with the mud as it dried, but because the colour of the mud helped them merge with their surroundings; covered in its red mud camouflage, an elephant standing still can be mistaken in the distance for a large red termite-hill, of which there were dozens in the vicinity.

But there is a lot to learn about elephants. Why are they "right-handed" when using their tusks? The right tusk is invariably used for digging with, and is the one which is more often broken.

To accommodate the weight of its tusks, an elephant's skull is large, though the brain occupies only a small part; and there is no doubt that elephants have smaller tusks nowadays, owing to the larger-tusked creatures being shot by hunters for trophies.

"This is what Slowly-Slowly wants," Ginny was saying. "This earth's quite different from that at the bungalow. Finer mud and a larger amount of it. It's just like a smooth paste when you mix it with water."

Bill groaned inwardly, envisaging the job he was being let in for. But it was back to the bungalow and to work, the business of wallow-building again. The mud of the right consistency was found, none of your gritty, hard stuff, and in a record two days the new wallow, Special Red Mark II, was completed.

"Who would have thought," Bill mused, "that an elephant could be so fussy about the kind of mud used?"

He barely got out of the way when Slowly-Slowly got the message and this time came charging over and stomped into the wallow.

But Ginny was sure it was worth it all, just to see Slowly-Slowly so happy. The new wallow, Special Red Mark II, was a riotous success.

"Lovely and squishy," Ginny laughed, as Slowly-Slowly slid forward and lowered his belly into the delicious red mass.

"Squishy—?"

"And squoshy—"

"Squoshy—?"

Ginny nodded enthusiastically. "Squoshy."

Slowly-Slowly began rolling over and over in the wallow with ever-increasing enjoyment. Soon she was "squishing" and "squoshing" not only herself with mud, but splashing both Ginny and Bill.

Bill began to suspect that Slowly-Slowly, "accidentally" flinging lumps of mud in their direction, was in fact broadly hinting that she was trying to involve him and Ginny in her mudlarks. It was then that Ginny had another idea, and, she thought, a better one. What Slowly-Slowly would enjoy most of all after a wallow was a swim.

The following day she and Bill, followed by Slowly-Slowly, went off to the river.

"It's a strange feeling, walking with an elephant," Ginny said to Bill. "Suddenly you feel sort of cut down to size."

By now Kadengi and Eleanor had got the idea and come swishing out of the bushes and followed Ginny and Bill with Slowly-Slowly, down the dusty road.

They reached the river. The other elephants had

gone; Slowly-Slowly and the other two had it all to themselves. The three of them were quickly enjoying every soggy moment, "splishing" and "sploshing" about in the muddy water, using their trunks like hose-pipes, squirting themselves and each other. They played together like happy children; Kadengi and Eleanor allowed Slowly-Slowly, who was sometimes in danger of half-drowning when she got into waters a bit too deep for her, to climb onto their backs and fool around, enjoying their own particular elephant games.

Then, the sunset was reflected in the pool, the surrounding trees were silhouettes, and birds began to settle on the river and feed. The African night fell over the water. Followed by their three friends, Bill and Ginny strolled contentedly back to the bungalow.

(2)

It took only a day or two for the bush telegraph to inform all sorts of animals and birds in the neighbourhood that there was a welcome on the mat at Tom Woodson's bungalow. Ostriches arrived to take a look at Bill and Ginny; several wart-hogs appeared on the scene, bringing with them a large number of baby wart-hogs. They chased each other, grunting, with their tails stuck straight up in the air.

But although Bill and Ginny were thrilled by their arrival, the ostriches and the wart-hogs, and other animals and birds, they were glad that Eleanor and Kadengi, and, of course, Slowly-Slowly were never far away. They found nothing so agreeable as their evening stroll with Slowly-Slowly, who had now become their specially dear friend.

And as they got to know her and Eleanor and Kadengi better, they wanted to learn more about other elephants. In the early mornings they would make excursions into the bush. Watching the wild elephants became a daily treat.

Who, apart from man, were the elephants' enemies? It seemed that adult elephants were not vulnerable to any foe. They never put themselves in a position in which they could be attacked. Scenting danger before it materialised, they were ready on their feet to move out of its way. But the young ones, because they had to lie down through sheer exhaustion from their long treks for food and water, were often in danger. Bill and Ginny observed that it was only with the greatest difficulty that a baby elephant could get up again once it had lain down.

One morning, visitors to the bungalow included some baboons. They were not far from the three elephants. One pair were picking up bits from the leaf-covered ground and eating them. Another pair were searching each other for dry skin, for the salt it contained. Then Bill and Ginny saw a bushbuck move through the grass, and Ginny remembered that some African tribes believe that because they were often to be seen playing together, the bushbuck and baboon were related.

Although this seemed unlikely, what did seem likely was that they provided an early-warning system for each other. This was demonstrated later when Bill and Ginny saw a leopard leaping from one branch of a tree to another—at once some nearby baboons started chattering their warning and both they and the bushbuck, who was feeding a short distance off, hurried away from danger.

It was on that occasion that, as the leopard rushed after the bushbuck, a lioness came running past the baboons, who were watching the leopard stalking the bushbuck. Then a whole pride of lions came through the grass. Immediately the leopard went up to the top of the tree, where he watched the lions as they majestically padded beneath him. At this moment Bill caught sight of a second leopard seated in a tree-top watching the lions.

This was typical of wild Africa. There was always someone watching someone else. It was a life of opportunism, a sudden chance to kill and to survive. Bill commented that the leopard knew he was safe enough up in the tree.

"Do you think so?" Ginny asked.

"Well, I mean," he said, "how many times do you see a lion up a tree?"

Even as they were moving away, Ginny glanced up and saw a lioness lying on a branch. But she decided not to mention this to Bill. A little further along, she saw a male lion also spread out along the branch of a tree. But still she did not mention it to Bill.

They drove back to the bungalow, and there was Slowly-Slowly as usual, to greet them. Trunk waving from side to side and making faint rumbling noises of pleasure, she ambled forward to greet them in her usual fashion, pushing and nudging against them with her head.

"It's just like having a very large house-dog," Bill said, patting Slowly-Slowly's magnificent pate.

Chapter 11

(1)

EARLY that evening, Slowly-Slowly took a wallow, which she shared with Bill, so that the latter soon felt he was somewhat in need of a bath himself.

Bill went into the little bath-house which stood on its own, away from the bungalow. He ran the water into the bath and sloshed himself thoroughly while he sang "God Save the Queen," really the only song he felt he sang rather well. Suddenly the door opened and Eleanor, attracted by the sound of Bill enjoying a wallow, decided to investigate and poked her trunk into the bath with the object, no doubt, or helping him benefit from her not inconsiderable experience in wallowing.

"Eleanor," Bill shouted. "Get out of here—"

But Eleanor pressed forward and proceeded to suck up the water.

"Eleanor," Bill shouted more loudly, "get out of here, go on—push off—"

But Eleanor was too busy sucking up the bath water while at the same time tickling Bill's feet. Now, she started to give herself a shower, throwing the bath-water over her back.

"Go away," Bill yelled. "This is private—it's a man's bathroom—it's not—I mean, you can't do that sort of thing—" He broke off. "Glug—glug—glug—" was all he could now utter, his mouth full of bath-water, as Eleanor squirted a trunkful at him.

Eleanor had reduced the bath-water considerably; now she emptied it completely as she turned another trunkful upon Bill, spraying him thoroughly. He gasped under the impact of the well-directed shower.

He was still gasping as she decided there was nothing more left in the bath and left him to towel himself in the muddy, watery wreck of a bathroom.

It was later, while she was preparing supper, that Ginny realised there were only eight more days to go before she and Bill would have to return to England. Through the kitchen window she was watching with amusement Bill working on the landrover just outside the bungalow. Eleanor, no doubt anxious to make up for having wrecked the bathroom, was attempting to lend him a hand. More accurately, a trunk.

She wasn't being very helpful in fact, and Bill, who was mending a puncture, was continually protesting that she ought to go and strip a tree, or even help Ginny with the supper.

Ginny encouraged him with the news that supper was almost ready. She added that they were down to their last thirty tins of beans. "Thank goodness," she said.

"Eleanor," Bill said, "go and find Slowly-Slowly." He had thrown Kadengi a motor-tyre to give him something to play with in case he should try to help mend the puncture too. Kadengi accepted the present graciously; but Eleanor remained persistent in her desire to give Bill her utmost assistance.

There's no doubt, Ginny thought, that Kadengi and Eleanor as well as Slowly-Slowly, have become more and more friendly and trusting. They seemed to consider themselves part of the family. And there *were* only eight days left, she reminded herself.

She sighed as she realised how lonely they might feel until Tom Woodson got back. Then a thought struck her. Supposing he was delayed? He might be delayed for a day. A week, even. A month. And all that time Kadengi, Eleanor and Slowly-Slowly would be on their own.

What would their reaction be, left alone after they had been on such friendly terms with Ginny and Bill? There ought to be someone to keep an eye on them, see they didn't wander off where they might be killed by some hunter. Or poachers.

There was a sudden cold feeling in her heart.

She had heard tales of the Liangulu, a small tribe about whom so very little is still known; a strange, mysterious bush people who did not even possess an official identity, about whose origins the anthropologists knew next to nothing. They were a people whose obsession and livelihood was the hunting down of elephants. They had, over the years, how long was unknown, massacred elephants to supply the tusks for the illicit ivory trade on the coast.

They killed with the bow—a weapon as old as the human race itself—the big bow, as it is known to hunters—which, until recent years, few white men had seen. Nearly six feet tall, these bows required prodigious strength to draw. The bow-string was made from giraffe leg sinew; and the arrows were poisonous, the heads fashioned from a six-inch nail fitted into a shaft three feet in length, with vulture wing-feathers for the vanes.

The poison used was based on a toxic ingredient derived from the acokanthera tree. There are several species of this tree, but the Liangulu seemed to prefer the muriju, bushy, with dark green leaves, sweet-smelling white tubular flowers and ovoid, purple-black berries. To the poison-brew were added ingredients possessing so-called witchcraft properties. These included entrails from puff-adders, crocodiles and a live elephant-shrew. The long-snouted elephant-shrew was highly important in the Liangulu's estimation. It hops about at night, invariably keeping to paths through the forest and bush—paths which, it was believed, the hunted elephants, stricken with a poisoned arrow, would follow. Accordingly, the Liangulu could follow and catch up with it when it died.

Armed with such a formidable weapon, the Liangulu hunter would approach as near as six feet to his intended victim, before letting fly, aiming at the liver, or kidneys, or the spleen round the side of the elephant's stomach. Struck by a freshly poisoned arrow, the animal could die in a few moments and there is no antidote. Though sometimes, especially if the poison wasn't fresh and therefore less potent, the victim could linger for hours, even days, before dying.

If the adult elephant has no enemy other than man, the baby elephant has many, including lions. Yet, strangely enough, the Liangulu played a necessary role in checking the elephant's proliferation, it has been argued. Had these hunters not perfected their methods, the prolific elephant could have overwhelmed the forests and plains of Africa. The anti-poaching campaigns served to put an end to the Liangulu poachers, but it gave them no occupation with which to replace their compulsive hunting of the elephant. An ethnic minority, as they had been described to Ginny, this unique people have suffered virtual extinction. While there is now, in fact, a continuing increase in elephants.

What an extraordinary, paradoxical twist, yet, as Ginny knew, there were still elephant-poachers operating on the same lines as the Liangulu. The thought of Slowly-Slowly or Kadengi or Eleanor meeting such a dreadful death at their hands made her blood run cold.

A sudden panic assailed her. She called out to Bill, who was still bent over the puncture. He heard her, but missed the note of panic in her tone, and without looking up he told Kadengi, who had given up playing with the spare tyre, to help her.

"Go and help Ginny," he said. "Or—or—something—"

Ginny was about to call him again; and then the line of her chin became firm, as she made up her own mind what should be done to ensure the safety of their three charges.

"Bill," she called once more. This time her voice was calm. This time Bill told Kadengi to go for a swim. Ginny was calling that supper was ready.

Yes, that's it, Ginny was deciding, they would go to George Adamson first thing in the morning—enrol his help.

(2)

And so it was that next morning, Bill and Ginny drove along the dust track across the bush country into the distance. It was a long, dusty drive to George Adamson, and they were thankful at last they sighted the sign-board: DANGER DO NOT LEAVE YOUR CAR. In a few moments they had reached the compound, where, resting in the shade of a tree, there was George with one of his lions. It was Boy. Bill and Ginny got out of the car, and walking across the coarse grass came George to greet them once again, with Boy rubbing his head against them in fond welcome.

Straight away Ginny and Bill put the subject of their concern about elephant-poachers fairly and squarely to George. They went so far as to suggest that he might like to leave his lions to do a spot of caretaking at Tom Woodson's bungalow until he got back from Switzerland. It would only be a matter of a day or two, they felt sure.

Their proposal was not over-enthusiastically received, which was not entirely unexpected. They knew George loved his lions. Ginny said lions were fine, but pointed out that wasn't it time George turned to other big game? And what could be bigger game than elephant? George took it all in his usual good-humoured way.

"You said your three elephants were all young— the way you describe them to me, their tusks wouldn't be more than twenty inches long. No self-respecting poacher would be after those. They want them about six feet long, weighing a hundred and fifty pounds, and more."

Bill and Ginny relaxed, his words had reassured them. George went on to suggest that if they left Kadengi, Eleanor and Slowly-Slowly as they found them, they would probably rejoin the herd to which they had originally belonged. The friendly three-some were hanging around the bungalow only be-cause people were there, George said. He was sure they would be able to fend for themselves when the time came.

As they talked Ginny and Bill followed George while he scattered bird-seed on the grass beneath the trees where the weaver birds were nesting. Small, yellow birds, they were flying about and darting into their nests which hung from the branches of the trees.

They build their nests, raffia-like cocoons, on the very tips of the branches, so that they cannot be reached by snakes, particularly boomslangs, which are thin and very poisonous. The weaver birds' green, hanging-basket nests, like seats on a merry-go-round, encircled the tree, making a picturesque sight against the clear blue sky. While they watched, Bill and Ginny saw one bird bring an-other a single blade of grass which the second bird took and then, as if obeying routine instruc-tions flew with it up to a nest. They saw squirrels hop down and take a share in the bird-seed George had scattered about.

George was definite that Kadengi, Eleanor and Slowly-Slowly would stay on at the bungalow only so long as Ginny and Bill were there to attract them. Otherwise, he felt certain they would have joined up already with a herd.

Bill and Ginny had learnt that George was usually right. He was that kind of person. He understood the birds and the beasts that sur-rounded his own private Garden of Eden. He had proved that it was possible to return to the wild lions which had been brought up in semi-captivity, and that the lions would rehabilitate themselves with other wild life.

Proof lay in his own pride which was constantly to-ing and fro-ing even while Bill and Ginny were there. The fence around his camp had been built not to keep his lions out, but to prevent other wild lions of unfriendly prides from walking in.

Beyond the fence Bill and Ginny could see several of George's pride lying under trees and in the long grass. There was Girl lying under one tree; Susua popped his head round another; and one-eyed Ugas poked his head up among the grass which hid the rest of him.

The alternative to George's scheme to keep a pride of lions living freely, would have been permanent imprisonment in a zoo—a negation of purpose, of life itself—something which Bill and Ginny knew was not the answer.

Ginny, together with Bill and George, went out into the long grass beyond the camp and sat beside Girl, stroking her. They had been such great friends in the days when they had made *Born Free* together, and Ginny was terribly pleased to learn that Girl was remembering and welcoming her again—after four years, and four years is almost a third of a lion's natural life.

Not far off, watching with deceptive disinterest were Girl's two cubs Mayo and Juno, born in the wild and never approached by human beings. They lay on the grass under a bush. Ginny and Bill hadn't seen them before. Bill went over and congratulated Boy, who was Girl's husband and also her brother, with a pat on the head.

"Husband or brother—that sort of thing doesn't

seem to count with lions?" Bill asked George. George smiled and shook his head.

Boy, now magnificent with a large, fairish mane, weighing over four hundred pounds, ruled the whole pride and kept the neighbouring lions at bay. Not without some scars, Bill learned when he patted him, not suspecting that he had a deep cut buried in the hair on his head. It was a tender spot and Boy gave a roar. He looked at Bill, kneeling beside him, and then rubbed his nose as if embarrassed at having given way to any such diplay of irritability. There had been no attempt at retaliation, only a warning.

While Ginny and Bill were renewing their acquaintance with Boy and Girl, one-eyed Ugas came onto the scene. Ugas was George's great friend. He was a little longer in the body, heavier and thinner than Boy, and a few years older. He possessed a dark brown, almost black mane and a very wrinkled brow. As he joined George and Bill and Ginny, he teased them all by nipping at their ankles playfully. But really he was the most friendly lion, the idea of his having even acted the role of a man-eater in the film *Born Free* seemed extremely incongruous.

Presently Bill and Ginny returned with George to his tent and they sat together, catching the smell of frying bacon which one of George's African boys was cooking.

By present day standards, life in George Adamson's camp was pretty basic—primitive almost, but as he sat there in his chair smoking a small cigar as a change from his pipe, Bill and Ginny couldn't help feeling that somehow he had found what the rest of the world was looking for. "Perhaps," said Ginny, "something that most of the world had overlooked in its hurry to get where it wanted to get to."

"And where's 'where'?" Bill said.

"Who knows?" Ginny answered. "Who knows?"

Chapter 12

(1)

GINNY felt totally reassured that the future welfare of Slowly-Slowly, Kadengi and Eleanor would be taken care of as she and Bill said goodbye to George Adamson and started back in "Mr. Mopagee" on their return to the bungalow.

They paused on the way to watch a hornbill, perched on a branch near a crevice in a tree-trunk. Bill was telling Ginny how, when the hen bird lays her eggs in the nest she has built in a hole in a tree, the male walls her up by plastering the entrance of the nest with mud, leaving only a narrow slit, through which he feeds her. She loses all her plumage during her imprisonment, until she is quite bereft of feathers, which go to line the nest. During the whole time she is hatching her eggs, she must rely on her mate for food. When she emerges, she is still minus any plumage and is unable to fly. She continues to rely on her mate for food until her feathers have grown.

Driving on, they were to witness a less appealing aspect of wild life.

They had been travelling through heavily wooded terrain, and were coming to the plains, when they first saw the herd of Thomson's gazelles moving across the grassland. At about the same time they came upon a pack of the most vicious animals on earth. The African wild dogs. Hungry, lean and ruthless, they are "the tough business-men of the animal world," as Bill described them.

He and Ginny realised that there were no other

animals about. Then they saw one single gazelle, alone, like a look-out—and so did the wild dogs.

Now, the dogs, irregular dirty black in colour, with white and yellow splotches, had got the gazelle's scent, also that of other gazelles nearby, and in a moment the chase was on. The whole pack was strung out as the gazelles turned together and headed off across the grassland. Very soon the dogs concentrated on the gazelle that had been acting as the look-out, and which had, in fact, been that much nearer the dog pack. The other gazelles had raced off, out of the way of danger.

While Bill and Ginny watched the dramatic chase, two dogs had got ahead of the rest of the pack and were now pacing the gazelle like runners in a race.

Time and again the gazelle tried to turn aside and make off in the direction of the herd, but each time the dogs managed to contain it in what was their territory. Now a third dog raced ahead of the other two, who dropped out. The third, fresher, dog was fast bearing down upon the terrified gazelle. It did its utmost to escape, but it was no good; it was tiring now. Then a fourth wild dog took up the chase as the third dropped out ofter a few yards. It lunged at its prey, caught it by the flank, pulled it down, and began tearing it to pieces. Within seconds, the whole pack had closed in, yelping and screaming, as they began to take the gazelle apart.

White-faced, Ginny turned to Bill. "Couldn't we have stopped it?" It had all happened so quickly; she had been mesmerised by the horror of the scene.

Bill put a comforting arm round her shoulder, and shook his head.

"They would have simply singled out another

victim. They're predators—like us, they need to eat each day."

He had noticed that unlike lions, the wild dogs unselfishly left the meat for the younger dogs to eat first. They kept guard while awaiting their turn.

Two hyenas appeared, one of them managing to snatch a piece of the wild dog's kill and race off. Some of the dogs chased after it and forced the hyena to drop the meat. The second hyena moved into the pack and grabbed hold of another piece of meat; but he didn't enjoy any better luck, and got his behind badly bitten before he could get away.

Then out of the sky the vultures swooped down. "Here they come," Ginny said, "the vultures— to tidy up." Soon the birds were clustered round the gazelle's carcass, gobbling up the last bits.

Soon there was nothing left except a warm stain in the warm earth.

Bill and Ginny were driving along the high street of a small town, more of a village, really, on their way back to the bungalow. They passed a corner restaurant which had hotel accommodations on its first floor, and "Mr. Mopagee's" rattling and coughing engine startled a white cat which was sleeping on the verandah.

They paused at a bazaar-type store, open-fronted, which displayed yards of gaily printed cotton, goat-skins, fly-swats, paraffin and a whole miscellany of goods, for sale. Ginny went in to buy some more picture postcards for Daniel, at home, and Nanny, and also to send to the children at school. While she was selecting the postcards, the Indian proprietor came up and endeavoured to sell her some monkeys on a bridge carved out of a single ivory tusk. He was very taken aback when Ginny told him sharply that she wasn't the least bit interested in some poor elephant's carved tusks, and she stormed out, quite forgetting her postcards.

She became somewhat mysterious about her next purchase.

She had been let into another little secret by Charles Matiso, and Bill couldn't think what she was up to when she waved to him and went into a general store which sold everything from curry-powder to chewing-gum. She came out with a package which, finally giving way to his curiosity, she unwrapped to reveal a number of pink lollipops.

Bill frowned at her, he couldn't imagine who on earth she had bought lollipops for. Not for him, of that he was sure. He found it impossible to resist remarking that Ginny must have got hold of the wrong end of the stick.

She remained enigmatic as they drove on, until at her suggestion Bill found himself stopping the landrover near the river, not far from Charles Matiso's compound. A few minutes later, the two orphan rhinos, Rufus and Rudy, arrived on the scene. Bill, still mystified, followed Ginny as she set off down the sandy track towards the rhinos, who awaited her with quiet expectancy—and then she produced the lollipops. Bill could hardly believe his eyes.

"Just a little goodbye present for them," Ginny said, as Rufus and Rudy took the sweets with every sign of appreciation. Bill stared open-mouthed at the two orphans demonstrating their curious manner of eating. They used their pointed upper lip to tuck each lollipop into their mouths. At crucial moments, it looked as if they had no upper lips at all.

Charles Matiso was away, but Ginny hadn't experienced the slightest feeling of apprehension as she fondled Rufus and Rudy; neither did Bill as he followed her example. Ginny allowed him to feed the rhinos with the lollipops. It was almost as if they were old friends, who had been expected to call again.

Not only did Rufus and Rudy enjoy the sweets, but they also swallowed the stick as well. In fact, Ginny felt convinced that the stick was the part of the lollipop they enjoyed most; anyway they were giving high-pitched, almost falsetto, squeaks as they tucked in.

But now, not only were the orphan rhinos taking interest in the lollipops, but the heads of several ostriches bobbed up against the clear blue sky watching intently what was going on; then a pair of buffalos and their calf formed an interesting party watching Rufus and Rudy with Bill and Ginny.

Ginny glanced around and gave an exclamation, pointing to the array of wild life watching them.

"It's like a mad Noah's ark tea-party," Bill said.

The ostriches began bending their necks and with their heads parallel to the ground searched for food. At the same time the buffalos began chewing grass. It was a spectacle not to be missed.

Two full-size rhinos being fed on lollipops, ostriches feeding like chickens and buffalos chewing the grass. "Just like cows chewing the cud," Ginny said. "They'll never believe this back home, if we were to tell them."

Bill nodded in agreement.

"We would be crazy even to try," he said, and then he and his wife burst out laughing. The lollipop sticks were sticking out of Rufus's and Rudy's mouths like cigarettes.

All too quickly the lollipops were finished, four dozen of them—the party was over. The rhinos wandered off, and Bill and Ginny continued on their way.

The morning arrived when Bill and Ginny went out for the last time in "Mr. Mopagee" just to reassure themselves that there were at least a few elephants within striking distance of Tom Woodson's bungalow. For Slowly-Slowly's sake and that of the other two, Bill and Ginny had taken to heart what George Adamson had said. They accepted his view that as soon as they went away Eleanor, Kadengi and Slowly-Slowly would find a herd to attach themselves to.

There were certainly plenty of elephants in the neighborhood; more than seventy adults, together with baby ones, one of the great herds in that part, and they were all within a few thousand yards of the bungalow, which was within a short distance of the river. As there was a water shortage, the elephants would be making frequent treks to the river, and so would be in the neighbourhood for quite a little while.

"Come to think of it," Ginny said, "it hasn't rained at all since we arrived in Africa."

Bill had stopped the landrover on the rough road, standing up in it, watched the elephants crossing the road. "Wonder what the weather's been like at home," he said. And Ginny knew that, like her, he had been thinking of the children.

Her thoughts came back to the three elephants at the bungalow. No, that happy, friendly trio wouldn't lack for company. Even if Tom Woodson didn't manage to get back the day she and Bill left. "Of course," she said to Bill as they drove back to the bungalow to pack, "it won't make it any easier to say good-bye to those—those three lovable idiots."

A little while later Bill and Ginny came out to see Eleanor and Kadengi taking a mud-bath in the wallow, joined very soon afterwards by Slowly-Slowly. Two hornbills on the branch of the tree watched the proceedings with interest, and a superb starling on top of a bush hopped about in excitement at the spectacle of the three elephants enjoying themselves in the mud.

Ginny laughed. "What a pity we can't take them back with us," she said.

"By plane?"

Ginny smiled at Bill. "How long does it take by sea?" she queried.

"For ever," Bill replied. He indicated Slowly-Slowly who was eating some leaves off a bush in the garden, having left the wallow.

"Well," he said with a grin, "if we haven't done such a great job of caretaking, she and the other two have certainly taken care of the garden."

"I do hope Tom won't blame us," Ginny said.

"We did all we could," Bill replied. "I mean, we kept the elephants happy—and Tom's an animal-lover, so he should be happy too. Anyway," he added, "I should think he must be used to this sort of thing."

"It is Africa, after all," Ginny said, "Not Surrey. . . . I just hope they won't miss us," she went on.

Bill put an arm around her shoulders reassuringly. "They'll be all right," he said. He wasn't going to admit how much he would miss them. Ginny found a slight difficulty in swallowing.

"We'll write to Tom as soon as we get home." She managed to get the words out with enthusiasm. "Yes, and ask if we can caretake next time he has an operation."

Slowly-Slowly left the bush from which she had been nibbling and came towards them. It was almost as if she sensed they were leaving, and Ginny wondered if the baby elephant and Kadengi and Eleanor would remember them next time, if she and Bill came back.

"I think they'll remember us, all right," Bill said, answering her unspoken question. "After all—you know what they say about elephants—"

He followed her into the bungalow. They picked up their baggage and came out. They paused to look at the three elephants, then they made their way towards the landrover. Slowly-Slowly and Eleanor stood watching them. Kadengi stopped eating the last remaining remnants of the flower-bed near the bungalow to raise his head.

Bill stowed the luggage aboard and he and Ginny got into the landrover. He remembered the routine and started to get out again, but this time Ginny stopped him with a smile. She jiggled the ignition key. Time, she thought, to let him into her little secret. He watched her, completely baffled. Nothing was happening. She jiggled the ignition-key some more, but still nothing happened. She stared at it, puzzled.

Bill looked at her as if the recent events had proved too much for her state of mind, gave a shrug and then fixed his gaze at the bonnet.

"Mr. Mopagee," he called.

The engine gave its little cough and started up. Bill and Ginny burst out laughing at each other and they drove off, turning out of the garden, to head down the road and into the distance.

Presently, they were driving along through green bush country, when it happened. There was a loud bang from somewhere underneath the engine, and "Mr. Mopagee" skidded to a stop. The landrover

[94]

ended up on the side of the road, steam pouring out of the radiator.

Bill jumped out, opened the bonnet, took a quick look, recoiled with a shudder, closed it immediately and whipped off his goggles.

Ginny, watching the fatalistic expression on his face, saw him move round to the back. She too, got out of the landrover. Bill was already taking out the suitcases, one of which he handed her with a little bow.

"Yours," he said, politely.

Ginny sighed deeply, took her suitcase and hold-all, and Bill collected his baggage together. They began to walk along the road towards Nairobi, taking a farewell look at "Mr. Mopagee," still belching smoke and steam.

They passed a signpost which said: NAIROBI 12 MILES.—when they heard a plodding noise behind them.

They could barely trust their ears. It couldn't be—? Yet the sound was unmistakably familiar. At last, they looked over their shoulders. Following them quietly, they saw first Kadengi, then Slowly-Slowly, and then Eleanor.

The sight momentarily halted them. Kadengi, Eleanor and Slowly-Slowly also stopped.

"Let's pretend they're a mirage," Bill suggested.

Ginny nodded. "Or a trick of the African light," she said. They continued on their way. The sound, which could only be the plod-plod of the elephants, followed them. Bill stopped again and glanced back.

This time there was no sign of the trio.

"They're gone," he said to Ginny.

As he pressed on, Ginny took a quick look over her shoulder. It was true—Kadengi, Eleanor and

Slowly-Slowly weren't there. It was a mirage—or a trick of the light.

She and Bill headed along the road to Nairobi, the sun beating down, a haze of dust rising around them. Then it came again, that plod-plod behind them. They stopped and swung around once more. They were there, again—Kadengi, Eleanor and Slowly-Slowly.

"I think," Bill said thoughtfully, "I get the idea. When we look at them individually, they're not there. When we look at them together, they are—"

"Which means," Ginny nodded excitedly, "that wherever we're together, they'll always be there, for us to remember—Kadengi, Eleanor and Slowly-Slowly—"

"And they'll never forget us—"

"And it means—oh, most of all it means," Ginny said fervently, "that we must come back—both of us."

"Don't worry, we'll come back," Bill said.